LAST TRACE

EMMA LAST SERIES: BOOK ELEVEN

MARY STONE

Copyright © 2024 by Mary Stone Publishing

All rights reserved.

No part of this book may be reproduced in any form or by any electronic or mechanical means, including information storage and retrieval systems, without written permission from the author, except for the use of brief quotations in a book review.

❦ Created with Vellum

For all who cherish the great outdoors—I may write about the dangers that lurk in the wild, but I hope you never lose your love for nature's beauty and adventure. May your journeys always be safe and your trails always lead to wonder.

DESCRIPTION

Sky above. Earth below. Trees around. Evil within.

With two members of the Violent Crimes Unit just out of the hospital and another still recovering, things are finally beginning to settle—except for Special Agent Emma Last. Her disturbing dreams of the Other are growing more vivid, and now a desperate fortune teller from a past case arrives on her doorstep. The woman's estranged husband took their ten-year-old camping, and they haven't been heard from in five days.

Are they lost? Or has the boy been abducted by his own father?

As Emma and her team investigate, they uncover something far more disturbing than a routine missing persons case. Four other hikers have recently vanished without a trace— until a severed foot is discovered, stark evidence of something far more sinister lurking in the wilderness.

As they navigate the fifteen thousand acres of unforgiving

wilderness, they encounter deadly traps hidden along the trails, meticulously designed to kill. This isn't just a man gone rogue—this is a predator, and he's hunting them.

The deeper they push into the woods, the more dangerous their mission becomes. There's a madman on the loose, and if they're not careful, they'll become his dinner.

Last Trace, the eleventh book in the Emma Last series by bestselling author Mary Stone, will redefine the concept of a hunger for revenge.

1

Burt Wilcox had been hiking since the morning, and his monthly solo excursion had gone well from the start. His husband, Charlie, was away for business, and Burt enjoyed his "me time" in the woods.

But now, with his energy rapidly waning, even after his lunch break, Burt had to admit the impossible.

I'm lost. How the hell did this happen? I never get lost out here.

Normally, he loved these trails. And their level of difficulty was just enough to give his middle-aged knees some exercise without risking agony or injury.

He stopped at a rise and leaned one hand against a tree, forcing himself to take a break. Ahead and behind him, the trail snaked through the dense forest, offering a narrow promise of escape.

Sticking a hand in his pocket, Burt ran a finger along the pocketknife he carried. A matter of habit more than necessity.

"In case you ever meet a mountain lion and need some help."

That was what Charlie had told him. Maybe joking or maybe not. As if a pocketknife would do a damn bit of good against a mountain lion. Burt had carried the blade as a good luck charm ever since Charlie gave it to him on their fourth anniversary. He'd even used it a few times…to open packages mostly.

Turning back to face the way he'd come, Burt eyed the wandering trail, spotting a boulder he'd definitely walked past earlier. In his youth, he'd gone up and down mountains with switchback trails and deep forests that had nearly spun him around more than he could count.

His sense of direction had always saved him, though. As well as his skill at reading terrain.

This is the northern hemisphere, so moss on a tree means that way is north. Spurs and draws come off a ridge, and following them up will put you on high ground, assuming your knees can take the climb.

Burt had hiked over three thousand miles in his lifetime and had never gotten lost for more than ten minutes. Except one time in college, when he'd been too stoned to pay attention. He and his friends got lucky that day, though, running into some veteran hikers who led them out, and he'd sworn off "hiking while high" ever since.

But today? Today, he needed a damn clue, a familiar sign to get him back on track, and he didn't see one.

"Screw it." Scraping with the knife, he made a wide mark in the moss on the boulder he'd walked by earlier. He'd start leaving some breadcrumbs.

His watch read two o'clock, which meant he'd been wandering these woods for upwards of five hours. Well, hiking for three or four, as planned. Wandering and realizing he was lost for a solid hour.

Before going on, he drank down some more water and pulled a few pieces of jerky from his pack. Biting into one, he kept on heading east along the trail. Earlier in the day, direction hadn't been all that important. The trails were maintained by the state and volunteers and had always been easy to follow.

Now that he'd wound up lost, direction was the one thing he could count on. The sun's rays slanted in through the canopy at Bernie's back. That meant he was heading east, and he'd be damn sure to keep going in that direction until he hit the park boundary.

Even if he found a fence that separated the park from private land, he could still follow that to a road and eventually get back to the parking lot and his car.

Or he could say "to hell with the rules" and go busting through the brush the minute he spotted a trail marker through the trees.

Trudging forward, he tried to figure out how this had happened. He was a careful man, always prepared. He had several survival kits he always kept in his backpack. In addition to an array of first aid supplies, one of the kits contained a solar charging brick, some flares, and an extra compass in case the one on his phone didn't work for some reason.

But when his phone had been on its last bar, and he'd searched his backpack for the charging brick, it wasn't there. Which was the moment he remembered that Charlie had taken it out after they'd traveled to Mexico last week, promising to put it back after charging the brick.

He must have forgotten. Burt had too. And just like that, the brick, flares, and compass were gone. He checked his phone. Nothing but black screen.

Dammit to hell.

Burt took a deep breath, refusing to panic. Charlie liked to kid him about being Grizzly Adams and never getting lost. He was in top hiker form, after all. Of course, not panicking was rule number one, and Burt was on the edge of breaking that rule in a big way.

But the thing was, he *knew* these trails. His senses of direction and familiarity were on his side when he'd started out that morning.

Maybe that's it. Maybe you got complacent. Got too comfortable and forgot to pay attention.

Another rise in the path loomed ahead, and he picked up his pace. The trees around the trail looked familiar. He'd swear he recognized the pattern of moss on one.

Burt stopped to examine the tree, but his attention was pulled down by a thick blanket of leaves that stretched out in an awkward line.

A purposeful and obvious line.

"You gotta be kidding me." He kicked the leaves away, revealing a trail, complete with tracks that matched his own damn boots. "Son of a bitch, who the hell's been messing with the trails?" Burt knelt and matched his boot treads to the tracks, just to be sure.

He stood straight, shifted his pack on his shoulders, and tightened the straps. "Hey," he yelled into the woods around him, "whoever's out there playing games, knock it off, all right?"

Gazing forward now, he could see how artificial the line of leaves and branches was. Someone had covered up the path on purpose and done it in a way that was sure to leave hikers chasing their own tails.

Stamina renewed—and more than a little pissed off at whoever had put him in this position—he stalked forward through the leaves.

Sweat beaded on his back. He slowed his pace, watching where he kicked leaves away and how he stepped. Breaking an ankle was the last thing he needed.

Behind him, the path stretched back to where he'd come from, but now he could see multiple trails shooting off in every direction.

"Shit."

He stalked back five feet, kicked some more leaves away, and uncovered more weeds. A few feet back, in the opposite direction, he uncovered a pathway.

What was he supposed to do now? Follow the path he thought was right, or trust his land navigation skills, meager as they were, and potentially end up miles from his car, or even on a hike that might take hours longer than following the trails?

The important thing was to make a decision. Give the trails a chance. An hour. See if he recognized the old routes. And if he didn't…rely on the sun's position. He took those outdoor training classes for a reason.

Number one rule. Don't panic.

He followed the path in front of him, dismissing the possibility that it could be another trick.

Whatever asshole had been out here messing with the paths, he hoped they woke up to food poisoning and landed on their ass for days. Or in the hospital. He hoped they'd still be slipping in their vomit or freezing in emergency rooms when he was already back home.

That was where he wanted to be. Back home, so he could get everything ready for when Charlie returned the day after tomorrow.

Burt always made a welcome home dinner for Charlie when he got back from his business trips.

Just have to get the hell out of these woods, get home, and shower. Then make a run to the grocery store in the morning.

His foot caught on a stick, and he reached down and tugged it up from the dirty leaves. He tossed it off to the side and spotted a structure tucked back into the trees.

A cabin had been erected out there, maybe twenty yards off the trail. Up a rise, but nothing he couldn't traverse by foot.

Abandoning the so-called path, he traipsed into the woods. His boots were solid, built for uneven terrain, and he moved fast. When he came up on a creek, he hurried his step and took a long leap over the bubbling water. On the other side, he used the momentum to keep going up the rise.

A path from the creek edge trailed through brush and bramble, aiming him at the cabin. Burt rushed on, one eye on his footing and one on the cabin, beckoning him forward.

Someone there would have a satellite phone or a vehicle, and he'd gladly pay them for a ride out of this forest. At worst, they'd know the woods well enough to get him out without any further delays, whether by foot or—

Stabs of pain, fierce and blazing hot, shot through his ankle. Burt howled as he fell forward, landing face down, his hands scraping across dirt, pebbles, and into a bramble patch beside the path.

A bear trap.

Screams ripped from Burt's throat as he twisted over, his backpack supporting him as he sat up. His ankle and lower leg throbbed in agony. He tried to lift his leg and cursed as the pain increased.

Rusted metal teeth ate into his jeans and the top of his boot. Dark blood spread from where the bear trap had snapped tight around his ankle.

"Who the hell leaves a bear trap out here? It's not even hunting season!" He gasped and screamed again as he shifted to reach for the trap. The motion put a strain on his leg that caused the teeth to dig in.

He stopped and remembered his wilderness first aid training.

Breathe. And don't panic.

Working not to move his injured leg, he leaned forward and reached toward the trap once again. He hadn't yet made himself touch the thing when the sound of branches breaking caught his attention.

Tears drawn up by the pain blurred his vision as he glanced sideways. A large man ambled toward him through the woods, slow and steady. A much smaller figure—a child—followed along a few steps back.

"Help." Burt's croak barely made it out of his chest, but somehow seemed to worsen the pain. Closing his eyes, he allowed himself to lie back in the leaves. "Help!"

The second plea sounded more solid, though it hadn't been needed, as he could hear the man and child coming his way.

"I think my ankle's broken." He looked up when he sensed a shadow looming over him. The man was big, his clothes filthy with dirt and seeped in some kind of dark liquid.

Blood.

"You must be hunters."

The man bent down by his ankle and fiddled with something nearby—pulling a branch from a tree for leverage, maybe—and Burt clenched his teeth, readying himself for the pain that would come when the teeth were released.

This would get worse before it got better, he knew.

The crouched man grunted. A tightening of something around Burt's leg, above the trap, drew him to look down.

A rope had been tied around his leg just below his knee—tight—but the other end of it rose up along the side of a large tree trunk.

"What are you doing? Is that…is that a tourniquet?" He pushed himself onto his elbows as the man did what Burt had expected. With his hands clamped around the edges of the trap, he worked it open. That sent another stab of agony through his wounds.

Burt fell back on the trail with an instinctive yell, hands back on the ground.

Mercifully, the trap's teeth came free, and the device was pulled down around his boot until his whole limb came free of the danger.

Working to catch his breath and thank the man, Burt breathed in deeply and exhaled. But when he looked back up, he froze.

The man had the long end of the rope in his hands—the end that draped down from the other side of the branch it was slung over.

He yanked down.

The rope bit into Burt's calf, and he was dragged upward in a flash. His ass came off the ground in another moment. Burt scratched at the forest floor for leverage—a tree root, anything—but the man was too fast, pulling him up and up and up.

"Wait! What the hell are you doing? Stop!" His pack tugged at his arms, gravity pulling it in the wrong direction and tightening the support strip across his chest. "Please, stop!"

The filthy man cocked his head, his expression buried behind a dirty beard that Burt now realized was also matted and sticky with blood. When the odor of the man suddenly caught him—raw, rotten meat—he fought not to puke while hanging upside down.

When the man reached out and released the chest strap, Burt's pack fell to the ground. It lay beneath him like a taunting prize he'd never claim. He fumbled for the knife in his pocket, but his hands were too slick with sweat.

The man's paw of a hand batted Burt's grasping fingers aside.

Behind the man, the boy was breathing fast, but saying nothing. His eyes were focused away from them, as if he might run in another direction. Or as if he simply didn't want to watch.

"Please, let me down." Blood rushing to his head, Burt felt himself swaying. The man tied off the rope to a low branch. He pulled a large hunting knife free from somewhere on his person. Upside down, for some reason, both the man and his weapon looked massive.

The giant reached out one hand to Burt's belt and gripped it, steadying him in the air.

Behind him, the boy whimpered. Like he knew what was coming.

That terrified Burt more than anything currently happening to him.

The knife came in close to his shirt, and Burt swatted at the man's arms, flailing as he tried to prevent what he knew was about to happen. The man balled his free hand into a fist and slammed it into Burt's stomach, taking the wind right out of him.

Saliva and bile filled his mouth, and he retched as his attacker tore his shirt down, slamming his fist into Burt's chin, cracking his teeth together and knocking his head back.

The most Burt could do in his precarious position was hold his arms across his midsection, now bare to the humid forest air and the animal with the knife.

A backhand blow spun his head to the side. Before he could even scream, the knife sank into his gut, like a lightning bolt seeking its target. Shock masked the pain, but only for a moment. Just as the first remnants of agony sliced through Burt, the man yanked the knife up with a wet, tearing rip into his sternum.

Burt's vision blurred red as thick, warm blood flowed into and over his face. But he could see well enough to watch in horrified shock as the man who'd just killed him licked the knife clean of blood with a satisfied smile.

A fresh wave of pain exploded through Burt as the man plunged a hand into his chest. A grotesque, wet squelch filled the air as fingers tore through flesh and muscle and into his very soul.

His vision tunneled, but he remained agonizingly aware as the hand emerged, clutching his still-beating heart. Burt's ears rang with the sound of his own blood rushing in and out of his body, now in the grip of another.

As he watched his heart pulsing weakly in the maniac's grasp, each beat a desperate plea for life, Burt's thoughts turned to Charlie. His heart was supposed to belong to his husband, to beat for him and with him. Memories of their life together flashed before his eyes. Their first date, the way Charlie's eyes sparkled with love, the plans they had for the future.

As the devil bit into his heart, Burt's last conscious thought was of Charlie's smile, a beacon of love and hope, now forever out of reach. All of it was slipping away. His heart, their heart, devoured right in front of him.

Mercifully, he didn't have to watch for long.

2

Emma ran warm water into the kitchen sink and splashed it on her face. No matter how many ghosts she'd seen, each appearance managed to startle her just enough that she wanted a shower. Preferably a hot one to chase away the deep chill of the Other.

The ghost of her neighbor, Mrs. Kellerly, paced her kitchen, muttering about how Emma needed to invite Oren over again soon. Which Emma could not do, since he'd been shot twice in the back and shoulder at his yoga studio by the perpetrator in one of Emma's cases.

She'd have thought Mrs. Kellerly would know that. But maybe ghosts didn't talk to each other much. At least, not as much as they did to Emma.

Gripping the edge of the counter, Emma sucked in a breath of warm steam. Then she bent an eyebrow at the old woman's white-eyed, translucent form. "Focus on inviting people who can attend Denae's get-well party."

At that, Mrs. Kellerly tutted. "You'll be no good to anybody as a spinster. Just look at me, why don't you?"

Emma put her hands on her hips and glared at the ghost.

"I am, and all I see is a ghost who'd rather poke into my private life than actually do anything helpful."

The ghost lifted her chin and scoffed before she disappeared.

"Good riddance, Mrs. Busybody."

With her gone, Emma picked up her phone and opened her notes app, where she'd been jotting down ideas for Denae's party.

Her colleague had narrowly avoided dying after being shot in the chest. She'd survived with the help of EMTs on the scene and a weeklong hospital stay, which she'd spent in a coma.

Denae's a fighter, and anyone who dares to say otherwise can come talk to me.

She'd take down anybody who had the gall to question Denae's suitability for the job of VCU Special Agent, but really, Emma knew the decision rested with Denae herself.

And she'd made her choice. She was taking a medical leave of absence with an indefinite return date.

Even with the uncertainty around Denae's status with the VCU, Emma, Leo, and the rest of their team were hoping to welcome their colleague home, and to celebrate her brother Jamaal's acceptance to art school.

They just needed the time to plan a get together. The idea of hosting a party put a momentary smile on Emma's face. Mia would be delighted to celebrate with them. She'd recently been released from her own hospital stay after her abduction and forced overdose on methamphetamines.

They'd all been through so damn much in the past few weeks, and Vance was still in the hospital recovering from a traumatic brain injury.

And just like that, any thoughts about hosting a party went right out the window. Celebrating felt like the last thing they should be doing.

But it'll give you all a reason to smile again, Emma girl.

A knock sounded at her door. Emma checked the time, immediately slapping a hand on her forehead. She'd forgotten Marigold was coming over.

And Emma hadn't even ordered dinner yet.

She hurried to let her psychic in and waved off the question brewing on Marigold's face. "You're not late. Or early. I just forgot to order dinner. I've been wrapped up, planning a thing for work. I hope you're okay with Chinese?"

Her brown eyes lit up. "I'll never say no to Chinese."

"Good." Emma sighed and shut the door. "I'll get that ordered right now. Go ahead and get comfortable."

Laughing, Marigold slid her shoulder bag off and let it rest near the kitchen island. Emma called up the closest restaurant and put in an order for their usual. When she hung up, Marigold was eyeing her with a grin. "Tea while we wait?"

"Yes. Sorry, I meant to have that ready too." Emma moved back into the kitchen and turned on the kettle, which she'd already filled. Tea was their standard fare on any night, so this much she'd been prepared for. "I'm a disaster in the kitchen. Always have been. Lack of practice, I guess."

The words had come off casually, but were only partly true, and Emma knew it. Distractions were everywhere lately, whether coming from her own brain or the Other.

Marigold eyed her as Emma put two mugs with tea bags on the island between them.

"I can do this much."

"You can do a lot," she countered gently. "But you need to give yourself some grace. Like usual."

Emma gave her a smile of thanks, holding her tongue.

"Catch me up, Emma." Marigold leaned across the island, her flyaway brown hair doing little to interrupt the intelligence radiating from her. "It's been a couple weeks since we sat down together. And you look like you've been through hell. I know you almost lost your colleagues, but I doubt the nerves I'm seeing are coming from grief or regret."

Emma opened her mouth to argue, but there wasn't any point.

So she launched into it, even before she'd poured the tea. "I've been dreaming of the Other, more intensely than before." She stared at the kettle. "I'm in the woods near where I grew up—"

"In the dreams? All of them?"

Emma nodded, forcing herself to slow down. "Near Salem. I'm hearing or seeing two women, but not as clearly as I would if it were real life. Sometimes, I can hear them without knowing what they're saying. And sometimes, I'm hearing that wolf howl, and it just gets closer and closer."

The teakettle whistled, drawing Emma's attention. She turned off the stove and brought the kettle over to the island.

Marigold held her mug out. "You said when you called that you've been hearing the wolf more and more lately."

After filling Marigold's cup, Emma poured boiling water into her own mug. "In dreams and when I'm awake, both. Sometimes, it sounds closer than others."

Marigold blew on her tea. "The Other is unpredictable. You know that. Oren may not always be available when you're ready for him."

The mug burned hot beneath Emma's hands, but she held the sides tighter. "I know. But it's not just that." She breathed in the scented steam, allowing it to warm her, and then launched into the worst of recent events.

How she'd damn near frozen to death while traveling to Boston, driving back and forth by Salem. How Leo had worried he needed to take her to an emergency room, the effects had been so obvious and terrifying. How she'd felt her bones trying to break apart.

"And yet," she sipped from her tea, savoring the burn on her tongue, "I feel like I do need to go back. Like I have no choice."

"You may not." Marigold brought her tea toward her lips, checked the motion at the heat, and placed it back on the island. "This Leo sounds like a good friend. You've trusted him with your abilities?"

Emma swallowed, feeling her cheeks warm. "I didn't want to…"

"But you did." The psychic reached across the island and gripped her hand. "And that's not a bad thing. You need to have someone in *this world* you can rely on. Someone who's around you more often than I can be, and who's more connected to your daily life."

Emma was saved from having to reply by the door buzzer.

She retrieved the food order from their delivery driver and carried it over to the island.

Marigold murmured her approval, and the two of them sank into the tastes and aromas, with Emma feeling as if she hadn't eaten in days.

By the time they'd scooped up the last of the fried rice and chow mein, Marigold was sitting back with a sigh. Her half smile made an appearance as she gave an exaggerated groan and stood up from her stool. "I'll let you clean up while I set up our séance. Is the living room all right?"

Emma waved the woman over to her little seating area. Shifting leftover containers into the trash can, she kept one eye on Marigold, who'd set to unpacking her shoulder bag.

The psychic laid a velvety red covering over Emma's glass coffee table before setting up crystals, not just on the table but also in various corners of the room. Incense came next, burning off to one side, sending curls of sage-scented smoke into the air. Four large blue candles completed the picture.

By the time Marigold dimmed the lights, Emma had washed her hands and moved into what now felt like an episode of *Hollywood Medium*.

"Is all this really necessary?" Emma watched as Marigold twitched her curtains closed, taking care to keep the edges of their fabric away from the lit candles set nearby on the floor. "Last time, I just sat here, and that was enough."

Marigold's lips thinned as she shook her head. "And last time, things didn't go as planned, did they? You dabbled in something you weren't experienced enough to control and got a shock."

Recalling her attempt at contacting the Other by herself, Emma shivered and looked away. In her memory, her mother's voice screamed a warning she'd never forget.

"Get out of here!"

She looked at Marigold again.

"Just temper your expectations, honey. After all, there are powerful forces in the Other, which have set themselves in opposition to you, and we both know it."

Even if weeks had passed, Emma didn't need to be reminded of what had happened. Trying to contact her mother had ended in one of the most threatening warnings she'd received from the living or the dead. "So where do I sit?" She wanted to move on from that memory.

Marigold pulled two throw pillows from the couch and placed them on the floor. She took a seat on one while gesturing Emma to the other. "We'll be more centered together like this. Near the candles and within the smoke. Take a seat, and then just stay quiet. Think calm thoughts, of your mother or Oren, but don't try to send a message. Trust me and relax."

Emma did as she was told, relaxing into the cushion. When Marigold put her hands out, Emma gripped them lightly and tried to dispel her nerves as the other woman began a slow, quiet chant.

Marigold went on and on, her voice slipping into a pleasant drone that barely penetrated Emma's awareness. Until the psychic's grip loosened on hers and the chanting ended.

Emma might've let go but for the chill in the room. Not the deep cold she'd felt outside Salem, thankfully, but the chill of the ghosts she'd become so accustomed to seeing.

When she opened her eyes, Marigold sat stiff across from her. Her eyes were iris-less, completely white, and all but glowed in the dim light. Emma's breath froze in her lungs, but she held herself back from speaking. The candle flames shifted erratically, flaring higher every few seconds, and the sage smoke swirled in the air, its scent growing stronger.

The delicious Chinese food from earlier spun in Emma's belly, and she again gripped Marigold's hands over the table. Waiting.

The psychic's lips moved, but no sound came. The candles flared higher, and the Other-cold stiffened Emma's fingers.

"Oh. Oh, my." Marigold breathed out and blinked, her brown irises returning. She shivered.

"Are you okay?"

"Get me some tea, dear. Please." Marigold nodded toward the kitchen. "I need to clean up to prevent any traces of the Other coming through. Especially those we'd rather not follow us here."

Emma's breath stilled. "Follow us?"

"Like they did when your mother warned you. Go now and brew a fresh batch of tea." Marigold stood and moved around the room, blowing out the candles.

Emma got to her feet a moment later and headed into the

kitchen. By the time she poured boiling water over the tea bags, Marigold had finished cleaning up.

"What did they say?" Emma's voice was soft, but the psychic nodded again, as if the question had been necessary.

"It's not that simple." Marigold held up a hand, forestalling Emma's complaint before it could come. "First of all, don't be discouraged by Oren's absence. I did not speak to him, but I felt him. I believe he's helping behind the scenes. Second of all, as to the women in the photos, I can't get a clear read on them, but I'm sure of one thing. Both women were your mother's best friends."

The photograph Emma had found made it clear her mother and the other two women meant something to one another. One of the three had written their collective initials on the back, with the message, *Eternally whole*.

"*Were* her best friends. Up until my mom died. Or did they have a falling-out before then?"

Marigold groaned. "I'm not sure, to be honest. Perhaps a little of both."

The ambiguity settled in Emma's heart, heavy as fog. "What else?"

"I'm sorry." Marigold shrugged, a fleeting look of helplessness crossing her face. "For tonight, that's the best we can do. But perhaps knowing they are, or were, friends might help? And if you're from Salem…"

Emma nodded. "Maybe they're from Salem and still there. And those pictures could help me find them."

Sipping her tea, Marigold seemed to settle in her seat. "I hope so. I think you need to try. To keep off the wolf, perhaps. And trust, meanwhile, that Oren means to do what he can for you."

Emma pushed herself up from her stool. "I think I have some Thin Mints around from the last few boxes I bought. How does that sound?"

The psychic remained silent for a moment, then agreed that cookies would be lovely.

Emma took longer than she needed to, going about finding them, as she struggled with the thought of her mother's best friends in life potentially being the ones her mother had warned her about in death.

The truth was like a blade hanging over her head.

Even with Denae back from near death, Leo knowing Emma's secret, the party they were planning…all of it paled in the face of what she knew in her heart.

She'd never been so alone.

3

Monique Varley's world vibrated around her. The little cabin she called home, in the woods outside Salem, was trying to knock itself apart. A vortex of violent howls whipped around her, causing the curtains to dance and her hair to flutter.

A picture jumped from the wall and landed at her feet, the glass splintering into a spider's web of shards. She shoved her hands tighter against her ears, but there was no muzzling the wolf that'd been accosting her day and night, whether she slept or woke. Whatever dreams she had, the endless howls drowned out everything else, and now they made the very ground beneath her feet shake.

I have to run. I can't stay here.

Despite the fact that her shack was protected, her charms would soon fail. She knew it. The wolf would no longer be kept away.

"It's getting worse." She shivered, stretching her numb fingers in the dark as the chill racked her body.

The howling and the wind faded in concert, circling up and away through her roof and into the night sky beyond. Careful to avoid broken glass and overturned plants,

Monique checked each window, ensuring the shutters were still latched tight.

A shiver took her as she confirmed her front door was secure. The same shiver had run through her just five days before, when she'd felt an involuntary connection to Emma Last.

Something had pulled on the young woman, as if trying to ensnare her and keep her trapped in Salem. And that same force seemed to be targeting Monique now, too, trying to put her off-balance, to weaken her. The howling sounded again, and she swiped one hand through the air in a warding-off gesture, clutching at the protective sachet she wore like a pendant.

Relentless, the howling accosted her senses. Monique needed to be cleansed, in body and spirit. Working quickly, she gathered the necessary herbs from her kitchen and went to draw a hot bath. She stirred the herbs into the water, allowing the steam to rise and fill her senses, all the while chanting her protective mantras.

The steaming water rose around her as she slipped into the tub. She embraced the heat, fighting off yet another shiver as a wolf's howl sought to puncture her protective envelope once again. Some part of her still felt the force of the wind, and she half expected the bathroom walls to crash down around her, leaving her exposed and vulnerable to her enemy.

Monique worried she'd somehow alerted that enemy to the cabin's location. This home, this place of power, should've been safe as long as she remained close. But what guarantee did she really have?

Her training and her connection with the Other were shared by the very woman who'd caused her to seek and create a hidden refuge in the first place.

I need to find Emma. To contact her once and for all, face-to-

face.

4

Emma had just settled into her desk chair at the VCU when her work phone rang. She stared at it for a second before picking it up, as the phone barely ever had cause to ring, given the cell in her pocket.

At 7:45 in the morning after another sleepless night, a solicitor was the last thing she needed.

"Agent Last speaking."

"Agent Last, this is Nicole Duluth at the security desk. I have a woman here to see you. Should I send her up?"

Staring at the VCU doors like they might offer an answer, Emma tried jogging her brain to life, but apparently, she needed more coffee. "A woman?"

"By the name of Esther Payne. She says it's about that circus case, from January? I know you just got here. Do you want me to wait until you're settled in?"

The fortune teller?

With memories of last night's meeting fresh in her mind, Emma pushed her work aside and lifted a blank notepad from her desk drawer.

"No, it's fine. Escort her up, please. Thanks."

Nicole hung up, and Emma made her way to the break room, where she poured herself some fresh coffee as her brain spun back to the last time she'd seen Esther Payne. The fortune teller was in her thirties, if she remembered correctly, but carried herself in a way that made her look almost grandmotherly. Emma had avoided her like the proverbial plague during that case.

Whether or not her powers were for real, Emma hadn't wanted to take the chance that her own abilities could get outed. Not when she was still struggling with what to make of them. The fortune teller, thankfully, hadn't been central to their case, gruesome as the killings of the circus performers had been, so it had been easy to avoid her.

Emma swallowed the thought just as Nicole escorted Esther to the VCU entrance and waved in greeting as she opened the door for her.

"Agent Last!" Esther's white-blond hair glistened under the fluorescents as she hurried forward.

Holding up the hand with her coffee, Emma held her off with an even voice. "Can I get you some—"

"No, please!" Esther stumbled to a halt, putting one hand over her mouth. Her long blue-painted fingernails were chipped, though the color appeared fresh. "I'm sorry, dear. I'm so sorry. Here you are, offering me coffee, and I just snap at you like—"

"It's okay." Emma kept her voice even. Esther's blue eyes were wide and wet, as if she might burst into tears, and they hadn't even gotten started. Whatever the woman had to tell her, she didn't mean it to be casual. "Let's go to the conference room, okay?" She gestured her past the desks, over to the glass-enclosed room with a blank whiteboard just waiting for its next case.

As Esther nodded and hurried in that direction, Emma ducked back into the break room and grabbed two water bottles from the fridge. With her tablet tucked under one arm and juggling the water bottles and her coffee, she made her way to the conference room to join Esther, who had taken a seat near one end of the table.

It had only been about three months since they'd seen each other, but the fortune teller looked older. Bags hung beneath her eyes, and today she wore the mom jeans and pullover of a tired parent rather than her token bohemian skirt and shawls. The spring weather sure hadn't refreshed her. Instead, with the loss of winter, she'd paled.

Emma used her foot to close the conference room door behind her. She set down her coffee first, then placed a bottle of water in front of the other woman. The second bottle went down beside Emma's coffee as she took the seat across from Esther.

"What is it you wanted to talk to me about? Is this related to what happened at the circus?" Emma opened her tablet and pulled up a note-taking app.

The other woman shook her head. She reached for the water and opened it, holding in a sob.

Emma sipped her coffee as Esther gulped some water and composed herself.

"I'm afraid it has to do with my husband and my son. Nothing to do with the circus."

"Why don't you fill me in?"

"Yes." Esther nodded as she held in another sob. "My husband, Steven, and I are estranged. We divorced last year, and we have a son, Will. He's ten. I haven't heard from them since Friday."

Emma made an effort to focus on Esther's words and took minimal notes on her tablet. So far, nothing the woman had said would compel Bureau involvement, but that could change.

She's out of her head with worry. Maybe a sympathetic ear is all she needs. And it's not like you had a stack of work on your desk, Emma girl.

"Let's start with your husband's name, description, and so forth. Sound okay?"

Nodding, Esther launched into a flurry of facts. "Steven Payne. He's a lumberjack of a man, brown hair and a big beard, very unkempt." She seemed to calm as she related more facts about her husband, his age, height, and approximate weight. "It's been some time since we exchanged more than two words. Hello and goodbye, mostly."

Emma suspected the couple had shared more than just those two words. She waited, letting Esther compose herself and continue.

"We were never really good at communicating, but he's changed, and now he's taken Will and gone incommunicado. I don't know what to think, to be honest. His phone goes straight to voicemail, not that he always carries it when he's off in those woods."

"Have you called Will?"

The fortune teller gaped at Emma for a moment before collecting herself. "We didn't give him a phone. Steven and I could never agree on much, but we both wanted to keep our son from getting addicted to a device. We were going to give him one on his thirteenth birthday."

Emma sat back. "Esther, I don't mean to sound unsympathetic, and if you're proposing that Steven has kidnapped Will, the FBI can help. But I have to ask if you've talked to the police first."

"The police won't listen. They told me to call Steven's lawyer because it's a matter of custody. But it's not! I need help. *They* need…" Esther's hands waved in frustration.

Emma pushed the untouched bottle of water toward her.

"You said you haven't heard from them since Friday. Is that normal?"

"Five days?" Esther swallowed some water and then twisted the cap back on. "No. When they go hiking, it's just for the weekend. Will is due back by Monday, always. For school."

"And a delay like this has never happened before?"

Esther shook her head wildly. "I just know something horrible has happened." One hand went to her stomach while the other pressed into her chest. "*You* understand."

Emma flinched at the knowing way the fortune teller leaned forward, but she didn't have time to move before the woman reached out and gripped her hand, tight.

"You heard me when I warned you about the wolf, dear. I know you did. Please. I was right then, and I'm right now. Something bad has happened!" Emma tugged at her hand, and the woman seemed to realize what she'd done. She pulled away with a squeak of an apology and shook her head. "I'm sorry. But, please, you have to understand."

If the woman had been someone else, Emma might've disagreed, but her every instinct screamed that Esther was correct. FBI case or not, her situation demanded help.

"The path to the wolf is covered in innocent blood, and that is the path you must take."

Those had been the exact words Esther Payne had communicated to Emma, back in January on the grounds of the Ruby Red Circus. Emma couldn't forget them any more than she could ignore the desperate glint in the woman's eyes, so different from the cool conviction with which she'd communicated her message months earlier.

Emma took a sip of her coffee and pulled her tablet closer, poised to take down every note she could. "Tell me about the last time you saw your son and ex-husband on Friday. Let's start there."

Esther squinted at her, as if about to argue, but then she nodded. "Steven was always a little off, it's true. When we were first together, I just thought of him as deeply passionate." She turned her hands palms-up and shook them. "But the marriage was rocky from the start. And I chalk it up to that. I didn't see through the passion to the lack of stability in his soul. He was a mess, really. So intense that he couldn't control himself or his emotions when the slightest thing went against his plan. He'd fly off the handle, break things, get into arguments with strangers like a madman."

Emma held her gaze. "Did he ever hit you? Or Will?"

"What?" The woman's eyes went wider. "Oh, no! I'm sorry, I should've said that first." The fortune teller closed her eyes and shook her head, one hand clutching her temple.

Emma waited for her to collect herself and then pressed on. "It's okay. That's why I'm here, to ask questions. Just keep going."

"Right. Steven never hit me. Or Will. He wouldn't do that. But he also wouldn't see a therapist, no matter how many times I begged him. His behavior started to take a real toll on our marriage. He was going off on his own and taking long hikes in the woods." She pressed her lips together, her eyes wide. "He'd be gone for days and refuse to talk about what he'd been doing when he came back. I knew he wasn't with some other woman. He'd return covered in dirt and smelling of the wilderness."

"That doesn't necessarily mean he wasn't with someone else. You know that, right?"

Esther paused, staring at her hands, which she held folded in her lap. She looked up. "Steven loved me, for all his faults, and he loves Will, but he wasn't the man I'd fallen in love with."

Emma nudged the water bottle toward the fortune teller once again, willing her to drink it. She could practically see

Esther's pulse pounding from across the table. "It's good that he never hurt you or Will. That's important."

The fortune teller's eyes flashed as she drank down some water. "And it's why I know something's wrong. That man has faults, but he *knows in his heart* that Will is better off with me. I know he does. He might want me back, but one way or another, he'd never jeopardize what we've got left by breaking our custody agreement. For Will's sake."

"He's never missed a pickup or drop-off? Never asked to alter the agreement or skirt around any restrictions?"

Esther gave a rapid shake of her head. "Never. Not once."

Emma tapped out a quick text to Leo.

Are you in yet? Walk-in from a previous case. Need a quick ear if you're up for it.

Leo's response was immediate. *Jacinda and I just got off the elevator. Need to get settled. Give me a few minutes?*

Sure thing. In the conference room when you're ready.

Turning back to the fortune teller, Emma tried for a clearer sense of Steven Payne's demeanor. "Was he always on edge?"

"I suspect Steven had a rough upbringing, but he wouldn't talk about it ever." Esther's voice was quiet. "He settled into hiking and backpacking as a hobby and was often calmer after he returned. He didn't talk much in general, but I was used to that by then. I thought hiking helped him work through his troubles. For a long time, he'd only hike when I was home from the Ruby Red. Then, when Will turned six and we separated, he'd take him along. But they'd always check in before and after."

"And did they check in this time?" Emma glanced at her phone screen, seeing that Leo had replied with a thumbs-up.

"They did, before they went out." Esther sat a little stiffer. "I talked to Will. He was excited to go fishing." Her voice died on a little whimper.

"Take a breath, Esther. We're gonna figure this out." Emma waited.

"That was Saturday morning. They were supposed to be back at Steven's home on Monday morning. I wanted the police to put out an Amber Alert, but when they heard Steven takes Will camping all the time, all they did was call the park rangers."

"And you're sure something has gone wrong, beyond them getting lost?"

"Ha." Esther threw one hand up, a touch of the confidence Emma remembered sparking in her again. "That man wouldn't get lost in those woods if he was blindfolded and hooked up to an IV full of whiskey! He always hikes the same woods. That man is not lost, I promise on my soul."

When doubt settled in Esther's eyes, Emma pressed. "But?"

Esther shrugged, weakness bleeding back into her lips. "But Will's only ten. If something happened to Steven, then Will could be out there alone. Steven says he's teaching him survival skills, but they've only just started, and…"

"And Will's only ten." Emma spoke softly, feeling the mother's tension vibrating between them. As long as she lived, she didn't think she'd ever forget the fear in this woman's eyes.

Esther nodded, mouth pinched.

"If it were up to me, Will wouldn't see him anymore, and that's the truth. He'd miss the hikes, but he'd just as soon play his games or mess around on his skateboard. The courts feel otherwise, so we share custody, but I know something's happened."

"And the two of you don't have any other children?"

Esther nearly crushed the water bottle between her hands. "Well, Steven may. I can't promise you he doesn't, but Will's our only child together. I'll tell you that Steven always did seem to be hiding something from me. Not another woman. But an older child? It's possible. Why?"

Emma shook her head. "Covering bases, mostly. Sometimes an older sibling can come into a case like this and mess with the status quo, but it doesn't sound like that's the situation here. Will talks to you?"

"Always." Esther nodded, certain again. "Tells me all about their hikes, but it's mostly all hiking and firewood and building forts. Fishing. That kind of thing. The boy can talk your ear off, and his father talks so little, I guess he uses me to process and share his feelings when he gets back."

Emma made a note of that, though the idea worried her more. A boy like that would've found a way to call his mother.

"Five days is a long time to be out of touch." Esther paled, and Emma quickly shifted tracks. "That's not intended as a final word. Survivors have been recovered after being lost or stranded in the wilderness for longer than that, and from what you've told me, this is absolutely an issue for the Bureau to investigate."

"Yes, please." Hope flickered to life in the other woman's eyes. "Please do something."

"We take all reports of missing or abducted children seriously. I need to share what you've told me with my supervisor before I can make any promises, but don't let that discourage you. In all likelihood, we'll be in touch with the police and probably state troopers to launch an investigation."

"Oh, thank you." Relief poured from the woman as she reached forward and clasped her hands over Emma's.

"Is there anything else you can tell me that might help? Where do they do their hiking? Which trailhead do they use?"

"Buckskin Wilderness." Esther began digging in her purse

and pulled out an old, crease-worn map of northwest Virginia a moment later. Just seeing the green on the map reminded Emma of how big the Shenandoah Valley was and how this part of Virginia stretched right on into the Appalachians. Depending on where the father and son were, finding them wouldn't be easy. "I know what you're thinking, Agent Last. I can read it on your face, but look here."

Esther pushed the map across to her and pointed at little spots that had been circled in pencil.

Emma tapped the map. "Where's this?"

"Norell. That's the town where Steven lives, and where Will stays with him when they're not hiking. You go over here, not a half hour away, and that's the main spot he usually parks when they go up into Buckskin."

Emma pulled the map closer, staring at the wide-open space. It wasn't huge, not like she'd feared, but the towns on the sides of the forest weren't close together either. "And he always parks there?"

"Well, not always. But these are the woods he hikes. He likes Buckskin. Plenty of fresh water, easy terrain, and lots of little hidden spots for hunters. Tons of trails, too, so the park rangers aren't always underfoot." She blushed. "Well, that's what he says, and what Will tells me. I hear they almost never see any rangers when they're up there, not unless a storm's coming and they have reason to be extra vigilant anyway."

Emma eyed the wilderness, and Esther noted a few more areas where she'd known Steven to park. When the woman finally stopped speaking and seemed to deflate, Emma reached across and gripped her wrist.

"It's okay, Esther. We're going to figure this out."

Now she just had to convince Jacinda of the same thing.

5

Leo eyed Emma from his desk. She'd wanted him to join her, but he wasn't quite ready to talk to anyone yet. His gaze raked over the email open in front of him one more time. He took in the words, doing his best to digest them at face value and not read too much into Denae's tone.

When that didn't work and he felt yet another urge to throw something across the room, he went back to observing Emma and her guest through the glass wall of the conference room.

The light-haired woman sitting with Emma looked familiar, though he couldn't place her. Older than Emma, balanced like a bird on a wire about to fall into the wind, but intense as all hell. Like she'd come in for a purpose and wouldn't be leaving without it. Leo just wondered what that had to do with Emma.

He sipped his coffee and tried to focus his mind on his work. On his job. On things he could control. He closed Denae's email and opened one from Jacinda.

After ten minutes, he'd managed to do nothing more than skim over Jacinda's notes regarding their most recent case.

He and Emma had helped the Bureau office in Boston shut down a trafficking operation.

His gaze tracked down the list of remaining emails and landed on Denae's again.

As painful as it was to see her name alongside the subject line that read *Next steps*, and as much as it hurt him to read what she'd had to say—not even twenty-four hours after coming out of her coma—Leo just couldn't remove the message from his inbox. And he'd read it a dozen times since she'd sent it at a quarter past five in the morning.

Her email had begun plainly enough, and with her humor and wit in full force. He clicked on it. Leo's heart had been so full of hope when he'd read the first line.

It's good to be back among the living!

He'd choked on his coffee as it occurred to him that Denae might be more familiar with the Other now than even Emma could claim to be.

That thought might've inspired him to smile if the rest of Denae's email didn't carry a more somber tone. She detailed the next steps she'd be taking in such...academic terms. Almost cold and unfeeling.

To all my colleagues, without whom I would not be here typing this right now, I wish to convey my deepest gratitude and admiration. I must also let you know that I will be taking an extended and, at this time, indefinite leave of absence from the Bureau.

I need to spend some time healing and also focusing on my family.

Leo wasn't sure what hurt more, that she hadn't called first to let him know or that she'd left him unnamed. Sure, Denae had been in a coma for close to a week, but couldn't she have at least texted him first, given him a heads-up?

She just lumped you in with her "colleagues."

Maybe he was primarily motivated by the frustration of

not being able to talk to her directly. He'd been awake, staring at the ceiling, having spent the night tossing and turning with hopes that he'd get a phone call from her… when his phone chimed with her group message.

At the hospital the day before, when she'd woken up, he'd only managed a short conversation, and her parents and brother were in the room at the time.

Not exactly the moment for PDA.

Denae hadn't said much of anything except "hi." And the email this morning made it clear she needed privacy and would reach out when she felt ready to do so.

Emma opened the door from the conference room to their office area, startling Leo from his thoughts. The light-haired woman exited past her, but quickly spun and wrapped Emma in a hug. Surprise flashed on her face, along with something else. Apprehension?

Leo turned his attention back to his computer, offering them some privacy while Emma escorted her visitor to the elevator.

She returned a moment later and aimed a finger toward Mia's desk. "Wasn't she coming back today?"

"Jacinda said she has a psych eval to complete first." Leo closed Denae's email, archived it, and picked up his coffee. "Sorry I didn't make it into the conference room. What was that meeting all about?"

Emma shrugged. "Follow me to Jacinda's office. I'll explain there."

She'd already turned, and he obediently jumped up after her. Whatever this was, it had to be better than stewing in his feelings.

When they'd seated themselves across from Jacinda, taking up the chairs she kept for guests, Emma shifted into a summary of her meeting.

Immediately, Leo remembered the fortune teller.

Because she was in more contemporary clothes and out of context, it might've taken days to place her face, but now that Emma put a name to her, he remembered her quiet humor and the way she'd talked about the circus victims. Acting as if they were family and making him believe it too.

Emma completed her debrief, and they both waited for Jacinda to reply.

After Emma handed her a map, Jacinda stared at where she'd laid it across her desk. "Five days is on the outside of what I'd call 'hopeful.' But you were right to advise her that we'd take it seriously. Don't go traipsing off to the wilderness right off the bat. Follow up with the police and get back to me."

"Thanks, Jacinda." Emma grinned, standing and taking the map back.

"Your choice, Leo." The SSA pointed to a pile of folders on her desk. "Paperwork or help Emma with her puzzle."

He tried not to let the surprise show on his face, but Jacinda only laughed.

"I have the paperwork in hand. You two take the puzzle."

Leo turned and followed Emma back to their desks, where she laid out the map once more.

Like Jacinda had said, it didn't offer much. They had some vague ideas of where their missing father might've parked his car before venturing into the wilderness. None of the trails were marked, since the map was too high-view for that and not designed for hikers, and if there were any service roads venturing into the trees, they weren't marked either.

Leo tapped a finger on the label, *Buckskin Wilderness*. "I'll dig into the forest first, while you check with the police?"

Emma sat down at her computer. "I'll double-check that the park rangers haven't gotten anywhere first. Could save us time if they already have people on the ground looking for the Paynes."

Leo turned to his own screen. He started with the basics, which weren't hard to find. The Buckskin Wilderness was super remote, but mentioned everywhere because it was also absolutely massive and peppered with trails that had been cleared, grown over, cleared again, and rerouted endlessly over the years. Leo soon found himself reviewing a log of people who'd visited and come back to report their experiences on a popular backpacking site.

Most of the comments talked about relaxed hikes, the remote atmosphere...exactly what he would've expected. But plenty of them also brought up the messiness of the trails. He slowed down to read one recent comment in detail.

Bring a map and compass! People get lost here all the time. The trails are hard to follow, and I swear it feels like some asshat's out there messing with them for kicks. Probably pot growers trying to hide their operation. Get in and out before sunset!

If people were getting lost "all the time," then park rangers would have more than a customary plan of action when someone was reported missing. They'd have developed a system to maximize the chances of rescuing lost hikers.

Emma was on the phone, leaving a message, so Leo checked for missing persons reports that mentioned Buckskin and sat back in his chair when the results popped up.

"Four disappearances in the last year alone." He whistled, looking at the dates on the reports that came in after that.

Emma ended her call with a grunt. "Park rangers are short-staffed and underfunded, but they located Steven Payne's vehicle in a parking area near the trailhead Esther pointed out on the map."

"No sign of them or a struggle?"

She shook her head. "Nothing at all. Just a truck left

parked where you'd expect if the driver went hiking. With a child missing, they got a warrant pretty quick. Forensics is already going over it. You get anything?"

"More than I'd hoped for, which isn't good news. Four missing persons cases in the Buckskin Wilderness in the past year alone. Compare that to a total of three unrecovered missing persons in that area the whole decade prior."

"Shit. That many people going missing could mean a drug operation got started out there in the past year. If hikers stumbled onto a grow site, they might have been disappeared to keep the operation hidden."

Leo nodded, but his focus was on the computer. "None of the hikers who disappeared were ever found. But one of them, a Lenny Faulkner…his foot was."

"His what now?"

He angled his screen to allow Emma to view the picture of two young women standing at the side of a trail with a park ranger. They read the article together in silence.

Two hikers discovered a human foot within the western stretch of Buckskin Wilderness. DNA tests have matched the remains to a Lenny Faulkner, who had been reported missing two weeks prior while on a solo hike. The rest of his body is yet unrecovered, but he is presumed dead due to animal attack, given the dismemberment of the intact foot.

Emma pulled up police reports around the death. "They never found him, but this seems a little clean, doesn't it? For a bear attack?"

Leo leaned sideways, unsurprised to find the foot in question at center-screen on her computer. As she'd said, it was too clean by half. He pointed to the ridges of skin along the ankle. "Practically straight. I've seen fish filets cut more ragged than that."

Emma raised an eyebrow at him. "Seriously?"

His skin warmed. "Sorry. The point is, I agree with you. I'm no expert, but that doesn't look like an animal attack."

More like a saw.

Invariably, his mind flashed back to old Boy Scouts trips and the saws they'd used to cut up firewood.

He stood up, already reaching out to fold Emma's map. Leo had a feeling they'd be needing it. "Let's take this to Jacinda. It looks like we have multiple missing persons and at least one body mutilation that likely led to death. With a child in the mix, we're talking federal joint task force."

6

After Emma called for the M.E.'s report on Larry Faulkner's foot, her phone chimed with the incoming email. She brought up the report on her tablet and printed out the picture of the foot before venturing back into Jacinda's office. Once there, she laid the image and report on the SSA's desk without fanfare. Beside her, Leo leaped into summarizing their findings, and Jacinda's eyes narrowed as he finished.

"You're telling me three people disappeared and weren't found over the last *decade*, and now it's four over the last year? Plus this latest father and son?" Jacinda looked like she might say something else, but a knock sounded at the door behind them before it shifted open.

"I'm here!" Mia gave a little wave. Her face wasn't nearly as sallow as the last time Emma had seen her, laid up in a hospital bed and attached to monitors. Still, Mia seemed more jittery than excited. "Just got cleared. Sort of." She looked at Jacinda. "I'm on desk duty, I think."

The SSA nodded. "Just until we're caught up here. I could use an extra set of hands."

Emma hurried around Leo to give her a fast hug. "How do you feel?"

Mia pulled away and returned Leo's embrace in turn, then leaned back to the door as if she needed to consider her answer. "I mean, I'm glad to be back. I just…" She gestured helplessly, her gaze drifting over to the bank of desks where they'd normally have been sitting with Denae and Vance.

"It's hard to be back without the full team." Jacinda settled back in her seat, though her fingers still played along the edge of the photo. "But maybe this will help. Emma, would you do the honors and catch Mia up?"

Emma directed Mia's gaze to the photo. "Does that look like an animal attack?"

"No. No, it doesn't. What's this about?"

Jacinda had begun dialing a number, and Emma summarized what she and Leo had learned so far. Mia had her tablet out and was taking notes when the SSA held up a hand to cut the conversation short. "Hello, District Ranger Ben Carter?"

Nodding, Jacinda introduced herself and asked if she could put him on speaker.

"Thank you. My team is here with me. We're hoping you can tell us everything you know about a reported animal attack a few months back. This is regarding the recovery of human remains belonging to Lenny Faulkner."

The man on the other side of the line breathed deep, and when his voice came back on, he stumbled. "Faulkner. Yeah. He, uh, was presumed dead by animal attack. But…"

The silence stretched on, and Leo leaned in and put his knuckles on the desk in waiting. Emma didn't blame him. If this man had been a witness in an interrogation room, he'd have been sweating bullets and on the edge of giving them a primary suspect or case-closing confession.

"Agent Hollingsworth, I guess I should ask why you're calling," he finally said.

"We're calling because the photograph we have of Mr. Faulkner's severed foot doesn't look like any animal attack we've ever seen. To clarify, the Medical Examiner's report indicates that Mr. Faulkner's foot was severed by mechanical means."

"Right." The man breathed deep again, clearing his throat.

Jacinda's fingers tightened on the edge of her desk. "Did you have more to add?"

"Uh, we looked for him. Searched the area like all get-out, but never found a body. Only makes sense that a bear or a pack of coyotes got to him. There's lots of wild animals in the area, and people sometimes set steel traps out there. He might have gone off the trail and stepped in one. Like I said, we looked for him and found nothing."

"Are you still looking for him?" Jacinda's question hung in the air, but they all knew the answer before it came.

"Buckskin is over fifteen thousand acres of wildlands. You have to understand, we'd need an office four times our size to really do our duties—"

"So you're not searching anymore?" Emma hadn't been able to hold the question back and only shrugged when Jacinda scowled at her. Someone had needed to ask.

"Uh, we are when we can. I can alert you if we find anything, or if you want to send some agents down here, the help wouldn't be turned down. 'Specially if you're looking to prioritize Faulkner's disappearance, as I figure he's long gone to the saints or the devils by now."

Mia hissed under her breath. "Charming, isn't he?"

Jacinda waved for quiet. "We have a development that I believe your office is aware of. Steven Payne and his ten-year-old son, Will Payne. They were reported missing earlier this week."

"That's true, and we did get a phone call from a woman by the name of Payne. Edith—"

"Esther. Her name is Esther Payne."

The man grunted. "That's right. I remember her calling and talking a mile a minute. Had to ask her a dozen times to repeat herself, since she was talking faster'n I can write."

"Did your office take action based on Mrs. Payne's report?"

"We did go out and take a look for the father and son, but…it's like with Faulkner. There's more land and hikers out here than my office can handle. It's just me and one of my rangers most days. Are you saying there's a larger effort getting started to find that man and his boy? Because I'll take all the help I can get."

"Yes, that's exactly what I'm saying. We've been asked to look into it, and with a child under the age of twelve involved, we're taking this seriously." Jacinda glanced up at her agents. "Have you put out and Amber Alert yet?"

Silence stretched for a tense moment before Ranger Carter replied. "We understood from the mother, Esther, that her husband often took the boy out on long hikes or overnight trips. The vehicle was right where she said it would be parked, no sign of foul play or mischief, even. She insisted something was wrong, but we ruled out abduction, and—"

"We're not ruling it out. My team will be there this afternoon. Hopefully, you'll be able to show them the ropes."

The ranger sighed. "We'll lay out the welcome mat."

Jacinda ended the call. "That settles it. You two get your gear and head on down there."

Emma had been about to turn away but froze for a half step. "Two?"

Mia had read the intent, though. "You were serious about desk duty."

"Just until I'm caught up a bit." Jacinda's expression softened. "Emma and Leo can investigate for now. You're with me."

Leo grunted, but patted Mia's shoulder in consolation. "We'll save any coyote wrestling until you get there."

The SSA folded up the map and passed it over to Emma. "See what you can find out from the rangers, and make sure you pack your hiking boots. Mia and I will dig into the other missing persons cases, as well as Steven Payne's background."

Mia's pinched face drew all the more attention to the effects of her ordeal. She'd nearly died alongside Denae at the end of the case, and Emma understood her need to get back on the job and put it all behind her. Emma gave her a smile. "Leo and I will get the lay of the land for now. You'll be back in the field soon enough."

7

Emma pulled into the park rangers' station in Norell, Virginia, glad to be getting out of the SUV again. They'd stopped at a diner off the freeway for coffee but waited so long that the grease in the atmosphere seemed to sink into their skin. To add to it, their to-go coffee had been weak. No help at all.

Leo grimaced as he rounded the vehicle. "We smell like French fries. Think we'll attract some bears after all?"

"In this place?" Emma glanced around the small parking lot and fought not to reference the wolves they were both all too familiar with. Tall, dense stands of trees surrounded them. "We should go back in time and have salad before leaving Washington."

Laughing, Leo headed for the door to the ranger station and held it open for her.

Inside, they were greeted by a long, narrow room. A table on the right displayed a detailed map. On the left, a couple of desks sat covered in folders, empty coffee cups, and bulky computer monitors that should've been replaced a decade ago. A gray-haired man behind the closest desk stood up and held out his hand. "District Ranger Ben Carter."

A trim, thirtysomething woman in uniform came through the door behind the desks, leaving it open.

As he handed Leo a folder, Ranger Carter pointed in her direction. "This's Ranger Laurie Mason."

Emma offered her ID to them both before pressing on. "I'd like to talk to you more about Lenny Faulkner."

The man waved her forward. "Not sure what else I can tell you that you haven't already heard. We did what we could and then some." He sighed and moved back to the other part of the room, where he leaned heavily on a desk.

Ranger Laurie Mason stood beside him, frowning. "Our funding's bare-bones. And like it or not, people get lost in the wilderness sometimes. It's remote out there, and hikers know the risks."

Ranger Carter straightened, sighing. "I've got this, Laurie. Get your hackles down. These agents are only doing their jobs."

Emma resisted the urge to smile as the woman raised her hands in surrender and returned to the back room. "How long do you usually search for a missing hiker?"

"Twenty-four hours minimum. In the case of Lenny Faulkner, we searched for seventy-two hours when he first went missing and spent another day in the woods after that foot was found and identified." He rubbed his hand through his thinning hair. "Man had to be dead, wounded like that. Nobody argued when we called off the search."

Leo handed the ranger his folder back. "Let's talk about Steven and Will Payne."

Carter headed back to the file cabinet with his folder in hand. "I know the man vaguely but not well. And I know he's missing. After your SSA mentioned it, I did some looking, and the police now have a report. Filed by his ex-wife, I understand." He sighed again, turning his back to the file cabinet. "It's why I didn't object when your supervisor suggested y'all come down here. I don't want people missing any more'n you do."

He waved his hands helplessly, and Emma understood. She didn't like it, but she understood. Overseeing a wilderness area of Buckskin's size was a gargantuan task. With just himself and a single assistant ranger on his staff, Carter had to call off deeper searches.

"Do you know if Steven Payne, or the Payne family, has any enemies in town? Anyone Mr. Payne has fought with?"

"Enemies is a little dramatic for Norell." Carter scratched behind one ear. "I can tell you he worked in landscaping for at least a few years. Seems to me there was some kind of accident he had a while back. Maybe work-related? Nothing serious enough to involve us or the police, or I'd remember."

Leo had his phone out and displayed the screen to Emma and the ranger, showing a list of companies. "Did Payne work for one of these?"

"The Green Men, that's it." Carter pointed at the first name on the screen. "They did a yard near my place, and I remember him being on the crew."

Emma picked up her tablet, tucking it beneath her arm. "We'll check into them before circling back. Do you have a ranger who could show us around the outskirts of the trails, at least?"

Carter nodded. "Not a problem. Just let me know where. But I hope you find that man and his son before you get into the woods. The Buckskin's pretty unforgiving, 'specially right now with mama bears leaving their dens with their babies. Springtime's just getting into the wildlife's veins, and snowmelt's coming from upriver." He sucked in a hissing breath that whistled through his teeth. "I don't envy anyone getting stuck out in those trees for longer than they planned for."

8

The Green Men had an office located in a nearby suburb off the interstate they'd followed into Norell. Emma pulled up to the curb just a house down from the address they'd found, parking a car's length away from a trailer with shovels and rakes hung along its side.

They sat for a moment watching a trio of men in kelly green coveralls in the next yard over.

Leo aimed a finger in their direction. "I'm guessing the guy I talked to is over there. He sounded like he was outside when I had him on the phone."

The two of them hopped out and moved along the cheerfully painted trailer with the company logo sporting the proverbial little green men with giant eyes and antennae, no less, until they came to the crew working.

One guy, who looked in charge, stepped over. He was tall and muscular and wore a faded t-shirt with a science fiction show title on the front.

The other men continued to work on the sprinklers in the yard behind him. He stuck out his hand and nodded to each of them in turn. "Billy King, LGM's owner and operator. My assistant said to expect you. Sorry he couldn't save you the trouble of coming out here."

Emma glanced at the men in the yard, then back to Billy. "We were told Steven Payne works with you."

"Worked. Past tense." Billy leaned against his truck and shrugged. "He hasn't worked with us for about a year, and I asked my guys. None of us have seen him lately. I haven't talked to him in months. That's why my assistant didn't know anything. He started after the last time we saw Payne."

Trading a look with Leo, Emma considered the news.

Payne couldn't even tell his ex-wife he'd changed jobs. Then again, that wouldn't qualify as either "hello" or "goodbye" and might've triggered Esther to seek changes to the custody agreement.

"Can you tell us about the circumstances surrounding his leaving the company? Was he fired, or did he resign?"

"Oh, he quit. I might've canned him, anyway, but he beat me to the punch."

"Can you elaborate? What inspired you to consider canning him?"

Billy paused and looked back at his crew. They'd begun laying in another stretch of PVC pipe. "Steven used to do good work for us. But then he started acting off, way off." He took off his cap and swiped sweat from his forehead. "He got injured on the job. Andy there," he aimed a thumb at the men behind him, "he was backing up the trailer, and Steven wasn't paying attention."

"What happened?"

"He didn't press charges or anything. He seemed fine, just got knocked down and stood back up and kept on working, but things changed after that."

Emma blinked. "I'm sorry, did you say the man got hit by a trailer and then seemed fine?"

Billy let out an awkward laugh. "Now, when you say it like that, it sounds bad!"

Shifting beside her, Leo made a point of meeting the man's eyes. "Could you give us the details of the accident, please?"

Seeming to realize he'd been a bit too casual, Billy straightened. "Right, well, uh, we had a big trailer we'd rented that day. Andy wasn't used to driving it and hit the gas on reverse a little too hard and, of course, headed left instead of right. Backing up a trailer takes practice and skill. Banged right into Steven's ass and knocked him down. I got scared right off, thinking I'd have to deal with a wrongful death lawsuit or something, but he jumped right up, right as rain."

"Did he go to the hospital?" Emma pressed, picturing the scene a little too easily.

"Wasn't no need." Billy shrugged, not reading the judgment in her question. "He'd gotten scraped up some, falling on the road like he did, but what was he gonna do, go to the ER for some Neosporin and a bruised elbow? He said he was fine to keep working, we believed him, and he finished out the workday. Problem was…"

Billy trailed off, gesturing at his crew.

Leo cleared his throat. "Problem was what?"

"One of my other guys, Marco, he said Steven hit his head pretty hard. I was at a bad angle, so I didn't see it, but Marco, he's pretty observant. He's out sick this week, but he'd remember. He was insistent Steven ought to go to the hospital, but the man refused. And our guys have health insurance, too, so it would've been covered, but he wasn't interested."

Emma jotted down the details of the accident. "Did he ever get to the hospital, do you know?"

"Don't know. I told him to. He had a headache at the end

of the workday. Chalked it up to lack of water and the heat, but we all told him to go get looked at. That was a Friday, though. He was back at work Monday like nothing happened, but I have no idea if he went to the hospital in the interim." Billy rubbed the back of his neck. "He'd ignore us if we asked about the accident, and I didn't give it much more thought than that."

Emma stretched her fingers, feeling nerves creeping in. The man had revealed an awful lot for not having seen Steven Payne recently, and that alone told her they were getting somewhere. "Why'd you mention it if you weren't worried then?"

"Well, it seemed like the start of things going bad with him, is all." Billy crossed his arms, eyes squinting into the sun. "Something changed in him, soon after that. He'd always had a bit of a temper, but he got worse. Started acting weird, paranoid, and got angry a lot. You stepped in front of him wrong, he was as liable to clock you as ask you to move aside. I had to talk to him a few times and probably would've had to fire him if not for the fact that he'd been such a loyal worker, long as he had. So I kept putting it off. And then he just stopped showing up to work."

Leo nodded for him to keep going. "And when was this?"

"Like I said, near on a year ago. I don't know if he started working for someone else, but the way he acted on my crew…I don't know who'd have had him. I tried to check in on him, though. Went over to his house, and I knew he was home because his old truck was in the driveway. But he'd never answer the door, so I gave up after three, four visits." Billy hunched his shoulders. "Never went back."

"And you haven't seen him since," Emma finished for him. Billy nodded.

"Well, we appreciate your time." Leo passed over his card,

and Billy eyed it before slipping it into his pocket. "If you see him, let us know?"

"Sure will."

With that, Billy headed over to his crew and resumed helping them.

Emma pulled out her phone as they headed back toward their vehicle. As soon as they'd closed themselves into the privacy of the SUV, she dialed Mia and put the phone on speaker.

"Mia, you find anything new on Steven Payne? It sounds like he left this landscaping company about a year back."

"Nope." She fumbled something on her end, muttering to herself. "I can look into it and see if we can come up with another employer."

Emma sighed. "Let's check his medical records first, if you don't mind. Esther didn't know he'd changed jobs, or I bet she'd have mentioned it. He had an accident on the job and banged his head. Maybe got a concussion. I don't know if that would be related to his disappearance, but it might give us some insight into his behavior. And if there's a pattern of him acting erratic—"

"Maybe Esther Payne was right and something really is wrong. Got it. I'll call you back shortly." Mia ended the call, leaving Emma and Leo alone with their thoughts and the hum of the air conditioner.

Emma pulled away from the curb, thinking about how little they really knew. "How about we get some lunch? I can't get French fries off my brain. You smell like a burger shack. And we can go over what we know before we visit Steven's house."

Leo raised an eyebrow at her. "First off, right back at you, and secondly, only if you promise not to pull out those bear maulings."

"Promise." Emma hit the gas, but let off when Leo

flinched beside her. Tension filled her, despite the lack of clues. "I don't like how King's comments on our missing father lined up so easily with his ex-wife's. It sounds like something is really, seriously wrong with this guy. If Mia gets back to us with bad news, we'll have to put out an Amber Alert."

"Jacinda will do that for sure." Leo sighed, drumming his fingers on a knee.

Emma nodded, trying not to think of what she'd have felt like if she'd ever been lost in the woods with her father and he'd started acting violent or unstable. They'd never been close, but he'd been predictable. Easy to understand even at the worst of times, when grief had been trying to tear them apart.

That kid may be feeling more alone than you are.

She licked her lips and didn't dare glance at Leo in case he was thinking the same thing as her, that the stakes had gone up quite a bit with that one simple interview. Nodding to herself, she spoke as much to center herself as for Leo's benefit. "We'll find them. We've had harder cases together. What are some trees compared to serial killers and gangs?"

"Right." Leo squinted into the distance, chewing on his lip before he went on. "But that's assuming Steven Payne isn't actively trying to stay hidden. That's a big forest. If he doesn't want to be found, he might never be."

9

Emma and Leo stopped at the first eatery they could find in Norell.

Around them, the local café known as Tessa's Diner seemed so quiet, it was as if the walls were listening to their conversation.

Emma lifted another fry to her lips just as the phone rang. Mia's name appeared on the screen. "Hey, Leo and I are just finishing up lunch."

"I'd say I'm jealous, but Jacinda ordered us Italian, so I bet we have you beat."

If Jacinda was getting Italian delivered, she was either trying to cheer Mia up or apologize to her. But this wasn't the time to ask. "Bet that's not why you're calling."

Leo excused himself to use the bathroom.

Mia began as Emma drew patterns in her ketchup with another fry. "We dug into Steven Payne. Two things seem potentially important. First, after that accident you mentioned a year back, he did seek medical care and was diagnosed with a TBI." She paused, and Emma could sense the hesitation and worry across the phone.

Vance suffered a similar injury a few weeks ago, and he's still in the hospital.

"Mia, you know Vance is getting the best care available. He's going to be okay."

"I know that. I do. It's just scary reading about this stuff and thinking of him lying in that bed with the wires and everything connected to him."

Emma let her friend take a few breaths and find her rhythm again.

"Back to Steven Payne. Medical records show he left the hospital early against the advice of his doctor."

"You worked fast." Emma signaled a server for more water. "I can't believe you got a hospital to open up their records that fast."

"Child endangerment opens a lot of doors, but I don't know how much it'll really help you beyond knowing there's an official diagnosis on the books. Payne was supposed to return for a follow-up but never did. The doctor's notes indicate he expressed 'extreme paranoia toward medical staff that may be in conjunction with the injury.'"

"Huh." She smiled as the server refilled her glass, then sipped her water, thinking about the timing of Payne's injury and his altered behavior at his job. "If he already had anger issues, maybe even some latent mental illness prior to the TBI, all that together could still be affecting him, even creating a synergistic effect."

"That's where Jacinda and I were going next. We don't have records of him being treated for mental illness of any kind, but he could've been living with an undiagnosed condition."

Leo came back, and Emma signaled it was time to go. Thankfully, they'd already paid at the counter when they'd ordered. "Hang on, Mia, we're going to the car."

"Got it. I'll keep myself entertained with the rest of this *linguine al pesto*."

Laughing and comforted by her friend's lightened mood, Emma led the way outside. At the SUV, she and Leo climbed in, and she set the phone in its cradle, tapping the speaker button.

"Okay, we're back."

Leo leaned in toward the phone. "What'd I miss?"

"You're on speaker," Emma added to Mia.

"To fill you in, Leo, we were hypothesizing that all those issues Payne's ex-wife brought up, from anxiety to antisocial tendencies, could've been the result of undiagnosed mental struggles he was dealing with. It wouldn't surprise me to know a TBI could exacerbate something like that."

Emma wrote notes into her tablet, copying Mia's phrasing word for word, before responding. "You said two things might be important, though. The TBI and what else?"

"He's got a record." Mia paused for a few seconds, chewing. "Sorry, it's been too long since I've had good Italian. Okay. Payne was arrested on an assault charge a few months ago. He'd just purchased a ton of wood and building supplies and went at a parking lot evangelist with a two-by-four. Payne accused the guy of being a government agent spying on private citizens. The case got thrown out only because the evangelist refused to press charges."

Emma jotted everything down as fast as her fingers could type. "The C.A. didn't pursue anything?"

"Payne never made physical contact, hence only the assault charge, no battery added. He just swung his wood around and threatened the guy."

"And that was a few months ago?" Leo gestured to Emma's tablet. "You haven't stopped typing since we got in. Brainstorm?"

Emma kept her eyes on her screen, where she'd just

pulled up the basics of traumatic brain injuries. Like everyone on their team, she'd known about them and not just because Vance had suffered one. TBIs had been connected to major contact sports like football and hockey and were in the news more often, it seemed.

"Listen to this." She read out loud for Mia and Leo. "TBIs have a variety of side effects, including everything from impulsiveness, mood swings, and loss of communication to the more obvious possibilities, such as headaches and confusion." She clicked on an article titled "TBI Victims and Psychosis," which was nested under a tab for other resources. "TBIs can be the cause of psychosis or contribute to the development of psychosis, especially in vulnerable patients."

Leo sat back and breathed in and out. "If we're right that Steven Payne had some sort of undiagnosed mental illness, I think he'd qualify as vulnerable."

They both thought for a moment before Emma noticed the empty silence from the other end of the phone call. "Mia? You still with us?"

"Yeah. I'm here." The tension and frustration in her voice cut right into Emma's focus.

She's worried sick about Vance, and who can blame her?

"Vance is going to be okay. Just hold onto that. We're supposed to hear from the doctor later today, or at least this week."

Mia cleared her throat. "Listen, guys, I need to finish eating and then update Jacinda. She's been on the phone all morning and had a lunch meeting with the ADD. She just left the conference room...hang on."

The SSA's voice came over the line moments later. "Mia will fill me in on the details. Do you need anything from me right now?"

"Yes. A warrant to search Payne's house ASAP. This is absolutely looking like a case of child endangerment."

Leo held up a hand. "How about also getting a BOLO out for the guy, even though he might be hiding out in the woods? It can't hurt to have his face all over the news."

"Will do, and I'll put the Amber Alert. Head to Payne's address and see what you can find."

Emma confirmed that was their next step. "We'll go straight there. Warrant should be easy enough to get, yeah?"

"No promises, but with a child involved, I imagine it'll be a quick approval."

Emma had the engine started even before Jacinda ended the call. If their guy was having paranoid or violent delusions that had escalated since using a two-by-four to defend himself from a "government agent," they needed to reach Payne and his son before he made another error in judgment.

Especially if he made that error in the middle of an already unforgiving wilderness.

10

I looked Will in the eye, doing my best not to scare him. "We are father and son…and that's how we live out here. Okay?" I tried to speak quietly, to encourage him to reply, but Will seemed dead set on being mute. He needed to understand me, but my words kept going wrong. Across the firepit from me, he hugged his knees, all big-eyed and pale.

Gotta show him how to live out here.

I waved at the nearby cabin. "This is all you need, Will. And me. I will teach you how to live here. Okay?"

His brown eyes stared. He rocked on his ass. I fought not to scowl at him.

"Listen up. My old son couldn't learn. I had to punish him for it. But you…" I tore up some more paper, tossing it into the pit. "You will learn. It's simple, if ya focus. Now watch what I do."

More bits went into the pit. Little papers and branches that could…I searched my brain for the word but couldn't find it. When I gave up and looked at Will, I made sure he was watching me.

He shifted, gaze on the steel rod I rubbed against flint. "I know how to make fire. You use kindling—"

"Kindling!" My shout shot him back two feet, and I flinched. "Sorry. I was looking for that word."

His lips formed an O, and a little grunt came out of him. My son, already so smart.

"If you already know how to make fire, you should help." I kept working my tools, striking sparks. The boy didn't move to help, though. Maybe it would take time.

I should've been more helpful. But my words kept stopping in my throat or getting lost in my brain before I could grab them.

Easier to show him.

He'll learn. My other son was a nuisance. Not really family. But Will? Well, just look at him. I know he can survive out here. I know we'll be a father-and-son team, connected to nature in no time. He can do this.

But my hope was unrealistic. He still cringed and turned away from me like he wanted to run.

And he couldn't do that.

Not now that we were here. This cabin would be the perfect home. I'd seen to it.

The sparks turned to flames, and I pulled away. I pointed to the pile of sticks beside him. "Help now, son!"

He jerked where he sat, like I had scolded him. But it got him to move.

Slowly, he took one hand from his knee and picked up a stick. He inched forward on his ass. I waited for him to move faster, to move like a man instead of a snail. Finally, he pushed his hand over the little fire. It dropped, too close—

"Be careful. Stop before you get that close. Stop!" His hand froze, and I grabbed his wrist and pulled it up. "Do you want to get burned?"

He blinked at me, his eyes brown and wet.

"You'll burn yourself!" I spat the warning.

He cowered again, yanking his hand out of my grasp and jerking back until he sat five feet away from the fire and from me.

I fed the fire. Worries ate at me.

I didn't want him to end up like my old son.

Looking at Will, I studied his huddled form and tear-tracked face. His overpriced clothing that didn't look forest-tested. His shoes that nearly glowed against the soil. They were still pure white in places where the dirt hadn't covered them yet.

Will remained where he was while I rose and went to my pack. The meat was there, waiting for me. Back at the fire, I acted rather than spoke. It was what I did best.

I'd already built a spit, and now I shoved the meat onto it. Showing him how it was done. He watched my hands, but I couldn't tell if he took anything in. If he cared to learn. Words would fail me if I tried, so I made sure the meat was held steady and then hung the spit over the fire.

"It takes time." I pointed to the spit, to the meat, and then to the flames. "We'll watch."

Will's gaze shifted to my pack, to where I'd kept the meat, but he didn't speak. I had to get him talking. That would mean he could be shown how to survive. He had to respond. Maybe he was worried my pack didn't have enough for us to eat. "Hey, son. We have plenty. Lots to share, to eat."

He opened his mouth to speak, closed it, and finally opened it again. A whisper came out. "Lots of what?"

If he asks questions, that's something.

"Meat. For two."

He shuddered where he sat and leaned away from me. "I'm not hungry."

My chest went hot. I dug my fingers into the dirt and

clenched them, tempted to throw something at him, a mound of dirt. But he stared at me, and I couldn't give up yet.

"You have to move the meat." I shifted the spit, letting the flames touch the still raw parts of the meal. "Keep it moving. So it won't burn on one end and be raw on the other."

He shrugged, holding his knees again. "I have food in my pack."

I stared at him. The meat smelled good. And it was nearly ready.

He ignored it.

Maybe he wasn't ready for it. No more than he was ready to fully help me or speak to me. We'd work on it.

The food was almost done. I stood up and went to the front of the cabin, where I'd dropped his pack near mine. I found the jerky and nuts he'd brought. No more than a few meals' worth.

"Tonight…okay. Okay?" I moved back to the fire and dropped the baggies of food by his sneakers. He only looked down at them. "Just for tonight. I'll eat the meat I cooked. You'll eat bagged food."

He'll come to think like me soon. He'll connect.

I let the fire continue burning as I brought the meat to my nose and sniffed. It smelled done. Ready.

The first bite was hot, juicy, and tender. More tender than I might've expected, given the beast I had killed. The boy stared, so I grinned at him.

He jerked his head down, eyes on his sneakers again.

"Eat!" I yelled. The woods went still around us, listening.

Sure enough, Will picked up his baggie of jerky. He took one slice out and shoved it between his lips. Dry, dark, and salty, it wouldn't compare to what I was eating.

I tore off another bite, my mouth watering with the richness of the game as I chewed through it. This was why we lived in the woods, and this was how he would learn to live. Soon.

He ate the jerky slowly. Maybe he wanted to make it last, but the baggies would empty. The little bit of jerky and nuts he had wouldn't last. He'd run out, and then he would connect—and he'd prove to me that he truly was my son.

Like father, like son. It would happen.

Not soon enough, but soon. I could feel it.

In the distance, someone yelled. The boy's eyes shot in that direction, and he started to rise.

When I hissed at him, some bits spit into the fire between us. He huddled back down where he sat.

I recognized the cry we'd heard. That was the person I'd been tracking earlier. The hiker who'd been lurking nearby. He was really lost now, starting to yell like crazy.

I didn't know what he wanted. What anyone wanted.

Why they kept coming by my cabin was beyond me. I looked at Will and another thought went around inside my head.

The people coming out here are looking for Will. They want to take him, maybe.

"They can't." I bit off another hunk of meat, chewing it slowly as I looked at Will. He took out his second piece of jerky. "If they try, I'll stop them. Their lies have nothing to do with us. *Nothing.*"

Their threats meant nothing. No matter what they said they could do, I wouldn't allow it. They could threaten to hurt me or take Will away or call down all their useless power on me, but Will and I would win. Over them.

I'll see to it.

"If you hear them talking, ignore their lies. Listen to me. Okay?"

Will seemed to know I wanted to protect him from the strangers. He huddled against his knees, chewing his store-bought jerky. Yes, he knew. I'd have no patience for any threat to us. I would fight if I had to. Fight for us.

This was our home now, and we would not risk losing it.

"I'll be a good dad." I watched my son, remembering my own dad's lessons. "And I'll teach you like my dad taught me. First lesson, okay? Failure is not an option. Being weak is not an option. We have to fight for what we have and survive."

Now that we had our cabin, our safe place to live and cook and connect and just be us within these woods, we needed nothing more.

Nobody would take Will away from me.

11

Emma and Leo sat parked outside Steven Payne's house with a Norell PD squad car in front of their SUV. One cop sat in the driver's seat, while the other stood near the trunk, finishing a cigarette.

Her phone lit up with Jacinda's call, and Emma swiped the screen. "Are we in?"

Jacinda barked, "Yes," which came off extra loud in the confines of the SUV. "The warrant went through. You two are good to go." After waiting for nearly an hour, they all but jumped from the vehicle, with Emma snatching her phone from its cradle on her way out.

Leo retightened his vest, giving a fleeting smile. "The one good thing about child endangerment, I guess. Figured that would make things move fast."

Emma waved to the cop standing beside the black-and-white. "Warrant came through. We're going in."

He nodded back and put a hand on his shoulder mic. "I'll let dispatch know."

"There's an Amber Alert out on Will," Jacinda continued, talking fast, "with us as point of contact, so we'll be first to know if anyone spots him. I'm sending Mia down for support. The way this looks, you can use the extra pair of eyes, and she's been itching for fieldwork all day. Just let us know what you find." Jacinda clicked off on that note.

A moment later, Emma marched up the walk to Steven Payne's front door. Leo was at her side, with the two cops following behind them.

The driveway was empty but for oil stains. Between that and the dark, silent house, Emma felt sure Payne and his son were somewhere in the wild. But they had to check here first, and with any luck, something they'd find would narrow down what path to take into the forest.

Steven Payne's little home lacked any indication that its owner worked in landscaping. The shrubs lining the front of the house were overgrown, with weeds showing in the soil beneath them. More weeds sprouted through the cracks in the front walk and at the edges of the drive.

The walk led in two directions at the top of the drive, with the left branch going around the corner of the house to a screened-in side porch. Emma led the group in that direction and found even more evidence of neglect. The porch held weather-beaten patio chairs, rusty garden tools, and a tear in almost every panel of screen.

Moving back to the front door, Emma noted a patchwork of rot on the siding. A few shingles hung limply on a shrub, suggesting the roof was badly in need of repair as well.

She rang the doorbell and leaned close, listening, but didn't hear a sound. "Good soundproofing or the doorbell doesn't work." She pulled open the screen door and knocked as she announced their presence. "Mr. Payne, this is the FBI! We have a warrant. Open up!"

Waiting a count of three, she repeated the knock as well as the warning, but they got no response. She taped the warrant to the screen door.

Behind them, the cops readied a breaching ram. Emma and Leo stepped aside, weapons drawn and held at sul position as they brought the ram forward.

It slammed into the door and cracked the frame, but the door didn't budge.

Leo put up a hand to hold them off from trying again. "Let me and Emma head around the back, maybe get a look inside through a window. He could have braced the door with something."

He stepped away, but Emma had already taken the lead, moving around the corner and following the wall toward the backyard.

She got to the back corner and paused below a window while Leo caught up. Together, they rose and checked inside. She saw the kitchen, empty but for a swarm of buzzing insects hovering around the sink.

They continued around the corner to the back door. Emma tried the knob, but it didn't even wiggle. No fewer than four dead bolts held the door tight in its frame.

Leo moved back to look into the kitchen again. "I can see the door from here. It's got some serious hardware locking it up. Might be the same out front."

"What do you mean by 'serious hardware'? More than the four dead bolts?"

He came back around the corner and nodded. "There's a railroad tie sitting near the door like it might get used as a brace."

"But it's not in use now?"

"Nope."

Taking the lead again, Emma led them back around the house to the front entrance, where they met the cops and filled them in.

"The place is empty, but the front door's set to withstand a siege. We breach the back, then?"

Leo moved to the window by the doorway and braced himself. "The kitchen was full of flies, which either means nobody's inside, or there's a body we haven't smelled yet. I say we breach here."

The cops lifted the ram again and drove it at the hinge side of the door. After two strikes, they'd loosened it from its frame, but it still hadn't moved inward at all. Leo went to their vehicles and returned with a Halligan bar. They used it to pry the door away from the frame and pull it clear.

They were met with a musty-smelling waft of air and another railroad tie, which had been placed across the entryway, making it impossible to open the door by pushing or even forcing it inward.

Emma jerked her chin at the railroad tie. "This guy cares about his privacy."

Leo and Emma pulled on gloves before entering, gesturing to the cops to stay outside and keep watch.

They ducked under the heavy chunk of oil-stained wood and began clearing the house, moving in tandem from room to room.

The place was sparsely decorated and dank with emptiness.

In the living room, a threadbare sofa and coffee table were the only furnishings. The kitchen sat opposite the dining area and held a towering collection of dirty dishes in the sink. A swarm of flies circled it. Every cupboard was loaded with canned goods that suggested Steven Payne had been stocking for the apocalypse.

Leo grunted. "Man's readying up for the end of the world." He moved ahead of her, gesturing to a pantry that was stocked from top to bottom with bottled water and toiletries. "And then some."

Beyond the kitchen, they found a bathroom that smelled like mold, with stains in the shower to verify the damp stench. Two bedrooms were at the end of the hall. The first held a queen-size bed, a decrepit dresser, and a small flat-screen television layered with dust. Leo waved her on rather than flipping on the light. "Next room's more interesting."

The second bedroom was nearly empty, but Steven Payne had clearly put it to good use. Four standard card tables and a folding chair took up most of the space. A box of metal rulers and mechanical pencils sat open on one table.

Emma moved up to the messy workspace and tried to take it all in. "Weirdest office I've ever seen, I'll give him that."

Drawings littered the first table, and when Leo flipped on the overhead light, it became clear they'd all been designs or diagrams of a sort. "Looks like a hunting cabin." He then pawed through a trash can, pulling out more drawings. "More of the same here. They're not expert, but he probably used those drafting tools to make these lines. They're all sharp and marked with measurements."

Eyeing the various versions as Leo unfolded a few, Emma nodded. "He's been at this a while, working up his perfect plan." She arranged some of the diagrams beside each other. "Look at this. He drew the same cabin over and over again."

Emma shook her head, imagining the man sitting at the rickety card tables, endlessly scrawling, scribbling, and, finally, constructing the more precise diagrams.

"He was obsessed."

Leo began turning the drawings over, looking for any further clues, and Emma shifted her attention to the closet. Door open, it looked empty, but she bent to the floorboards and checked to make sure Payne didn't have any hidden compartments. When she stood, she ran her hand over the top shelf and was just about to give up when her fingers brushed against what felt like a block of wood.

She pulled at it, but the object didn't budge, as if glued

down. "Hey, Leo, give me a hand? Bring that chair over and steady it."

With Leo gripping the folding chair, she stepped up onto the seat—not the best stepping stool, she knew—and shined her flashlight into the corner of the upper closet space. Sure enough, there was a wooden block there, protruding from the wall at the back of the shelf.

Rather than tugging on it, she pushed, and it slid straight and fast into the wall. Something below clicked, and Leo whistled.

"Better hop down and look at this."

Moving the block above had released a trapdoor in the rear wall below, allowing Leo to push it in and slide it to the side. That revealed a smaller closet. Guns hung all along the back wall, with crates and cans of ammunition stacked below them. To the right, canned goods rose nearly to the top of the six-foot ceiling. On the left, a trio of shelves were stacked one atop another. Electric lanterns filled the first, a shoebox of batteries the second. On the top shelf sat a small, leather-bound book.

Emma grabbed the book, adrenaline spiking. "Eureka, maybe?"

The pages inside were filled from margin to margin, crammed full of tiny writing.

Emma turned back to the first page and read out loud. "I saw the government man again today, while I was waiting for Esther and Will. He had a special watch, so he could hear anything I said, but I didn't give him anything. Didn't even say hello to my own wife and son. Esther was upset, but she'd understand if she knew. The government wants to take us all down into their laboratories, and if I give them my voice, that's the first step."

She read farther down the page about how the government man wanted to "steal" Payne's voice and trap him underground and would do the same to Will and Esther if he allowed it.

Leo shook his head, reading over her shoulder. "The man's full-on delusional."

One entry ran into the next, with only changes in the color of ink to show the passage of time. Not a single entry was dated. Some repeated the same conspiracy he'd started with. Others spoke of plots to turn over "good citizens" to aliens for research or to use Virginia citizens as test subjects for various sorts of experiments. Still others ranted of nuclear winter, poison in bottled water, and a religious plot to turn everyone "fire-breathing" before it was too late.

Too late for what, Emma didn't know, and she shut the journal before she could find out. Leo opened it back up, muttering something about a clue having to be somewhere, but Emma turned away and moved back to the bedroom doorway.

The room had gone slightly chill, but she'd only realized it when taking all her focus off the journal. And now, she saw the source of the cold.

Back in the living room, the ghost of a hiker knelt in the entryway. Sunlight from the open door fell over him without having any effect, and Emma saw the two cops beyond him, keeping an eye out in the front yard.

She sidled up beside him and knelt in the cold of his presence, but he kept staring downward at what had once been his hands but were now see-through appendages.

Blood dripped from his sleeves, the man's arm bones, radius and ulna, poking out from beneath flannel and cotton. Torn muscle was in worse shape than his clothing, holding on by threads of gristle and tendon.

She hadn't seen a ghost missing part of himself, not this up-close, since Ned. His headlessness—or rather, his transparent head on top of his real-looking body—had jolted her senses all those weeks ago. Somehow, the ghost before her, who moaned over his own hands, was even worse. If only because he seemed so keenly focused on his loss.

The hiker shook before her, muttering, and she pushed herself to bend farther into the Other, going deeper into the cold to hear him. "He's insane. What does he want with me? Did he build this out here? He's insane. And he has my hands. Both my hands. They're his now. All his."

The ghost began wailing then, shaking so violently that blood dripped from his opened wrists faster. His jeans were soaked with it, but the blood and bits of muscle that fell disappeared into nothing.

Emma's lunch did a flip in her stomach. She hurried to stand as one of the cops came up to the door, speaking over the ghost's wailing to ask if she was all right.

"Fine. I'm fine. Just thought I saw something."

For a moment, she feared the ghost might've heard her and taken offense at the intimation that he wasn't real. But his wailing simmered down, and he began to repeat what he'd already said.

She made herself move backward, one step at a time, even as the cop outside looked at her as if she might've lost her mind.

In the bedroom, she found Leo staring at a U.S. Geological Survey map of Buckskin Wilderness hung on the wall. Computer printouts detailing conspiracy theories of disappearances framed the map. Despite the colorful highlighted markings added on the printouts, the map was what held Leo's focus.

"You find something?" She coughed, shaking the cold out of her hands and aiming to steady her voice.

He glanced at her, eyes narrowed. "You look like you've seen—"

"Yeah." She gestured back to the entryway. "I did, and I'll tell you all about it. But first, what's this?"

Leo pointed to several spots on the map. "I don't know what these Xs mean, but take a look."

Emma stepped up beside him and counted six red Xs placed in various spots. They were clustered over a single area a few miles in from the outskirts of the forest that butted up against Norell. "All of them are near water and within a few miles of where he could park."

"They must be spots where he was thinking of building that cabin. It's too late to search now, but…hey. Emma? Emma, are you all right?"

She wasn't, actually. Leo's voice had nearly faded into a faint shimmering of white noise surrounding her, and a chill had begun seeping into her, through her clothes and beneath her skin.

The air around her had gone frigid with the Other, but it wasn't like what she'd felt out in the entryway. This cold was more abrasive. Severe and extreme—like what she'd felt as they'd passed by Salem recently, but not suffocating.

This cold sank right into her bones, stabbing as if the Other were trying to kill her. The handless ghost swayed in the doorway with his white-eyed gaze focused on her. And then, another voice swarmed forth from him, not the one she'd heard just moments ago. This one assailed her.

"Emma Last. You took what was mine. And I will make you pay the price, someday soon."

Before Emma, the room rippled as her vision trembled, going foggy. She reached for Leo, but her hand fell on dead space as she stumbled forward, toward the ghost.

"Emma Last. You will pay."

The voice surged forward, but a second one rose against it in Emma's mind, simply saying her name. "Emma." With a warmer, less menacing tone, the new voice overpowered the first.

Emma's vision steadied as she met Leo's eyes. He was watching her intently, as if fearful that she might succumb to another shivering fit like she had on their drives through Salem last week.

She gazed around the room, ensuring they were alone, before speaking quietly. "I heard a voice, full of anger. Directed at me."

Leo moved in front of her, leaning in to meet her gaze. He placed a hand on her shoulder. "You saw a ghost? Or—"

"Yes, a ghost with no hands. But someone else was speaking through him just now, and another voice came from I don't know where, to fight him off or the spirit that was using him to threaten me." Emma spun, examining the room for signs of the Other. But the hiker ghost and the voices were gone, just as surely as the cold. "And I don't know who any of them were."

12

Monique whispered the rest of her incantation, closing out the ceremony while she still had the power to do so properly. Her whole body sagged with exhaustion, but finally, she'd made some progress.

The scents of rosemary, dragon's blood, and rue drifted around her. Carefully crafted bracelets circled her upper and lower arms with hematite and thorns. Additional protection, just in case. Even within a circle of salt that itself lay within her place of power and her most shielded space, this was no time to be lazy about keeping herself hidden.

If the battle she'd just fought was any indication, she'd need every bit of help she could call on to defeat her foe and protect Emma Last from harm.

Monique stood and took four deep breaths, blowing them out in each cardinal direction before exiting the salt circle. She then opened her eyes and considered what she'd learned.

The young woman looked so much like her mother, it brought tears to Monique's eyes. Even through the fog that had shaded her sight when she'd first come onto the scene,

Emma's striking blue eyes and light-brown hair had seemed like an updated version of her old friend, Gina.

Monique had entered the Other, through a ghost that was in the same room as Emma. Then the onslaught had begun, the attack no doubt encouraged by Monique's recklessness. First, the ghost Monique had inhabited locked up tight like a vise, squeezing her so hard, she thought her breathing might stop.

When that constricting feeling finally eased and Monique took in a deep breath, she wanted to scream at Emma to run, find safety. But she couldn't spare a second of attention for anything but defense.

Countless spirits swarmed around her vision, each of them attempting to push past her and escape the Other. Monique had almost let them do it, too, thinking they'd finally find peace after crossing over.

But she'd seen, just in time, what those spirits were attempting to do.

They wanted to attack Emma, to clutch at her and hold her fast.

If you hadn't intervened, they might've dragged her over. She might've been trapped in the Other forever.

Monique wouldn't make the same mistake again. She might have been protected here in her place of power. But reaching out across the Other, to seek out Emma and communicate with her, had opened a doorway.

And the enemy had wasted no time in charging right through it.

Around Monique, her room looked the same as it had earlier—neatly kept and ringed by crystals and herbs and candles—but it was sullied by the knowledge that after spending most of her life protecting Emma Last, she'd finally succumbed to the temptation to speak to the woman and had very nearly undone all the protective work of the past twenty-eight years.

She wouldn't think on it. Imagining the worst would do her no good, not now and not ever. Shifting into cleanup mode, Monique moved over to her washbasin and removed her bracelets before lathering herself with the oak-based protection wash she'd spent so much time making the day before. Perhaps that had been the reason she'd been able to defeat her foe so handily. She'd have to make more of it.

"So strange to see Emma through another's eyes." Monique shivered at the memory of Emma's haunted expression. She'd been focused on the form Monique had taken but was disturbed by it too. There'd been a bond there, though. Monique had watched Emma reading a journal in a mostly nondescript bedroom. There'd been papers and maps tacked to much of the wall, though she'd been unable to discern any details.

Perhaps the haze of the ghost's vision had been the reason she'd had such trouble seeing Emma at first. Even when the fog had lifted, Emma had needed to step closer before Monique had seen the details of her features and the shock of discomfort in the woman's eyes.

And that had been when the enemy chose to attack. The conduit had been opened for Monique to talk with Emma, but that opening also allowed hostile forces to assail her.

Monique began to make plans for what she'd have to do next if she wanted to have a more lasting protective effect on Emma.

She needed a stronger bond. And if communication was what opened the path for the enemy as well, Monique would wait for that to happen and make sure she was ready for that moment.

When Emma had enough ghosts around her for Monique to reach out more clearly, through a more grounded spirit who'd offer real connection, that would be the moment of power that would allow Monique to deliver her message and ensure she could protect Gina's daughter.

She only hoped it would happen soon, before the enemy found her own way into Emma's world.

13

The sun had already set, and Pat Henson was struggling to keep himself from having a full-blown panic attack.

Nothing was adding up, and some part of him wondered if he'd managed to poison himself somehow. Sure, he'd washed those mushrooms he'd found, and he'd eaten the same variety in these woods dozens of times before.

But dammit, I'm fucking lost!

He stopped in the center of what should've been the primary trail back to where he'd parked his car the day before, but his boots sank into a drift of leaves and branches. The trail app he used assured him this was the correct path, but how was that possible?

There is no damn path here!

Pulling out the folded map in his pocket, he braced it against a nearby tree trunk and shined his flashlight down along the trail, comparing what he saw to his own memory, the trail app, and the trails he'd been following—no, *attempting to follow*—for the last twelve hours and counting.

"Maybe the map's out of date, but the app gets updated all the time." He stared at the image on his phone showing where two main trails should've been intersecting, but his mind went back to the near-apocalyptic snowstorms they'd had that winter. Maybe the weather had been bad enough to force some real changes to the trail layout.

Still, the app would have been updated with USGS data since then.

Grunting in frustration, he folded the physical map and shoved it into his pocket. The thing was clearly useless.

He did a one-eighty and stomped back down the trail, thinking he must've missed the intersection point. Maybe a downed branch had misled him in the dark.

The wilds of Buckskin stretched out around him, but he traipsed forward with one eye on the ground and one eye on his phone. That wasn't the smartest thing to be doing, let alone at night, but he didn't want to be stuck out here until morning.

Panic edged up his esophagus, but he held it back. He'd shouted for help earlier and accomplished nothing but tiring out his throat, which he'd attempted to assuage with half his water supply.

I'm fifty-four years old, dammit. I've been hiking longer'n most of the hikers in these parts, and I'll still be doing it when they've moved on to glamping and talking about their glory days.

Still roaming in the brush, Pat swung his flashlight beam around, hoping it might catch on a bit of metal or a car windshield, anything that would tell him he was, in fact, heading back to where he'd parked.

He was certain he'd gone the right direction earlier, and his app told him he was near the trailhead.

"What the hell?" Pat's gaze caught on a clearing some ten feet away. He ran his flashlight beam around it and stepped forward, pushing between a stand of low shrubs and saplings. Beyond the stretch of undergrowth he'd been following, a trail stretched out as clear as day.

It wasn't a game trail, but a proper hiking path, cared for and just right for a human body passing through.

He looked down at his feet. A large shrub blocked his path and had been shepherding him back the way he'd come until now. Crouching, he played his flashlight along the dirt at its base.

Red-hot anger crept up his spine, and he reached out one hand to shove the shrub sideways. It toppled to the side, unconnected to the ground. In front of him now lay mounds of leaves and broken branches.

He stood and began kicking the detritus to the side, uncovering the path that had been so clear on the map and which he'd stomped on past because some asshole had made a point of covering it over.

"No wonder people've been getting lost." He hefted a large branch that had been laid over the trail and tossed it away into the woods. "And you better believe I'm reporting this sabotage to the ranger's station."

He moved faster now and breathed lighter when he reached the actual trail. His flashlight beam illuminated clear soil as far as it would reach, and he played it back and forth, as if making sure his eyes weren't offering up a hallucination.

Noise sounded off in the woods to his back. The sound of footfalls, he thought.

Normally, Pat wasn't an angry man, but the timing was too obvious. Whoever had sabotaged this trail—for shits and giggles, he had to assume—was traipsing about in the wild and laughing at him.

He turned toward the sound and roared his anger. "You could get someone killed like this, shithead!" The sound stopped, and he huffed for breath before turning back to the trail that would lead him out of these damn woods.

The last bit of debris was ahead of him, and he used the long side of his boot to sweep it aside. Instead of normal dirt, though, the movement showed a dark stain on the forest floor. Like oil blemishing the trail, thick and black.

He bent to it, sniffed, and froze.

In his younger years, he'd done some time volunteering for the Red Cross in disaster areas. The things he'd seen had chased him out of emergency response, but some things were so strong in his memory, he'd never forget them.

Like this. A coppery, dead-smelling patch of blood that someone had taken pains to cover over. Big enough to have meant the lifeblood had drained out of some poor creature, right where he stood.

Probably a bear. Maybe a big deer.

Stumbling to his feet, he worked to control his breath even as he hopped over the blood patch. Panic pushed his heart faster as he moved, a lump growing in his throat, but he focused on breathing deep and moving forward.

The dark woods and lack of supplies were getting to him, but he'd be fine now. He was on his way out.

That was animal blood. That's all it was. Some poor deer or bear that paused at the wrong spot and didn't listen to its nose.

But despite the logic, the sabotaging of the trail on top of the hours spent lost all added up to only one thing, no matter how he looked at them. He needed out of these woods, and it'd be a cold day in hell before he ever came back—

His ankle caught on an obstacle and sent him falling forward, just catching himself before his nose went straight into the ground. Before he'd had a chance to turn or even think of standing, branches pummeled him from above, falling around him as if some giant net of loose wood had been released on top of him.

Breathing in dirt, ankle throbbing, he lay frozen beneath the woodpile that seemed to have fallen from the sky.

When he pushed himself to his knees, his back felt like it might break from the strain, but he got to all fours and took in a full breath. Branches lay half on top of him still, and his heart pounded. He tried shaking himself like a dog to clear the wood, but his body wouldn't cooperate. One of his wrists gave out beneath him, and he rolled sideways, screaming with the forceful tear of something in his lower arm.

As ragged breaths ripped through him, thorns sank into his shoulder where he'd landed. Footfalls sounded not far off in the woods, but considering what had just happened, they didn't bring him any comfort.

Awkwardly, he rolled onto his back, landing on his pack. His flashlight was gone, but he felt the wetness on his arm and his leg, and he knew. Blood, and probably a broken wrist along with the ankle, the way both appendages were now screaming at him.

He looked up as a light bobbed from the trail near where he'd been standing when he'd tripped. A large figure played the light over him, blinding him. Using his good arm to try to sit up, he made it onto his elbow and panted for breath. "I need…I need help."

The light tilted down toward his feet, showing a broken ankle, a bloody gash, and a taut wire stretched over the path.

Pat's heart beat faster as the air in his lungs froze. He hadn't tripped on some rock. He'd stumbled across a fucking *trip wire* set up across a popular hiking trail.

The figure with the light stepped forward, boots picking their way between broken branches. Behind the man, a smaller figure—a child—stood staring on.

This isn't happening. This can't really be happening.

"Son, watch close now." The figure spoke slowly, seeming to struggle with the words. "I'm going to show you the easy way to make a kill."

14

The man's skin was soaked with sweat, smellier than our first kill, but his body was thicker with muscle. Healthier. Blood slithered out of his throat with a quiet gurgle, and my knife came out clean.

"A good connection." I wiped the knife against my pants, showing my son. He watched me, eyes dull, and I smiled. He didn't look away like he did on the first kill. It would do for now. "Look at the wire trip."

Get the words right for him, dammit.

"Trip wire. I meant trip wire."

The wire remained intact, and I ran one finger along it, making it shine with blood. That was fine…it would only make it harder to see against the soil of the path. The boy said nothing but stepped closer. Trembling. I reached for his hand, and he flinched, but I pointed down to the wire.

He crouched and touched one finger to a clean portion that wasn't tarnished with blood.

I grinned at him. "Good. Look." I traced my hand over the rest of the path, ignoring the body for now so I could show him the whole of the trap. "Okay? Up here."

The wire ran to the edge of the path, through an eyebolt set into the ground at an angle. That let the wire go upward, along the side of a hefty tree trunk.

I pointed to the loose hammock that had held the wood, waiting for the boy to see the design.

"The man fell. That fabric had the logs set to fall on him. The wire tripped, and the wood fell. See?"

My son shifted on his feet, still shaking, and I worried he didn't believe me.

"It's smart. Okay?"

Staring, he finally nodded. Lips barely opening to whisper, but he answered. "Okay."

I nodded. "And you can learn too. It also works on animals. Good meat to feed us. Yeah?"

The boy flinched, and I pointed at the dead man.

"He wanted to invade us. Nobody. Nobody can invade our home. Our cabin."

He'll get it. He's already said some words, more than the old son ever could. He'll get it.

Quiet now, the boy only looked at the wire. Tired of waiting, I swept my knife against my pants again, wiping away the excess blood. Then I stepped back to stand by the man's chest, and I held out my knife to him. "You do it. Cut his clothes off."

My son's eyes went wide, orbs of confusion, and I stepped toward him fast. One of my boots came down on the edge of his sneaker, anchoring his toes.

"Do it. Now!" My words echoed in the dark around us.

He finally took the knife from me and knelt.

Gripping the bottom of the man's pants with one hand, he pushed the knife up against the outside seam. The blade poked right through them and into the skin, but I didn't correct him. He'd learn.

His work was messy, but the boy drew the knife up and

split the pants. I helped him by taking the belt and the shoes off as he moved to the shirt, going all the way up one side of the body rather than finishing one piece of clothing first.

Not the way I would've done it, but okay.

A whimper came from him when he cut through the blood-soaked flannel. I ignored it. When the sound kept coming, I stared at him, and that fixed it.

He'd learn to be quiet. To live in the woods as my perfect son. Smart. Quiet. Careful.

The shirt work was messy and more complicated than it needed to be, but he finished. Blood all over his hands, he pulled one arm free of the fabric. Then the other. The undershirt, he cut up the side of the man, trying and failing to avoid the blood soaking through the dirty white fabric. The knife kept poking the skin, marring it.

Tattoos covered the man's pale skin with words I couldn't read.

My son finally got down the other side of the jeans, completing the task.

That was good. Messy or not, he'd worked for this cleaning.

"You are my son." The words were near a whisper, and he didn't react. Only tried to hand me back the blade. I took it from him, nodding. "You are my son. And it will get easier."

I looked over the fallen logs. The trap had worked just as I'd planned, but it would be a job putting it back together.

We'd take care of that tomorrow. Another lesson, another chance for Will to learn.

I moved to the man's chest, kneeling with my knife, and gestured for my son to kneel across from me. I noticed that he kept away from the blood pooled around the man, but we'd work on that. My son would worry less about things that didn't matter in the near future.

"Okay. We have big things…plans." I had to almost spit

the words through my lips. As my son got better at being my son, I would get better at speaking to him. "Big plans for this man. We are going to get to know him. Okay?"

The boy stared at me, trying to wipe the blood off his arms and hands by running them against his jeans.

I put a hand on his shoulder, and he stopped moving like he'd been caught in one of my snares. I put my other hand on the dead man's body. "We have to get to know this man now. The best way…only way…to get to know him, is to connect with him."

Will shivered in front of me, no doubt chilled by the wet blood staining his shirt and his skin. He'd warm up later with the fire.

"We join with him and connect, okay? *Connection*. That is good. Remember, son. Connection."

15

Just after sunrise, Emma pulled the SUV to a stop at the trailhead where Steven Payne's truck had been located. It had since been towed to the sheriff's impound, where it was being thoroughly examined for forensic evidence. With any luck, driver and vehicle would be reunited by the end of the day.

That's assuming the driver and his ten-year-old son are still alive.

District Ranger Carter, Ranger Mason, and another man wearing outdoor gear, waited beside their vehicles.

Mia leaned forward from the back seat. "Which one's Ranger Rick?"

"Huh?" Leo met her gaze in the rearview mirror.

Emma chuckled as she hit the door handle. "Old reference before *any* of our times, Ambrose."

Mia pouted comically, arguing as they all got out of the vehicle. "*Ranger Rick* magazines never go out of style, I'll have you know. Take my advice, Leo, and get some back issues for those nieces of yours."

Emma let them quibble behind her as she walked forward, greeting Ranger Carter with a handshake.

Circles beneath his eyes suggested he hadn't slept much since seeing them last, but he forced a smile. "We got a call last night. Hiker by the name of Pat Henson didn't get home when he planned. Wife's in a tizzy."

"You starting a search?" Emma looked beyond him to the other rangers at the back of a department SUV. They looked to be organizing packs.

"Not for Henson. At least not yet." Carter gave a perfunctory nod to Mia and Leo as they approached. "Hasn't been forty-eight hours, and the man's grown. For all I know, he could be mad at his wife and wanting some peace 'n' quiet. Wouldn't be the first time."

"But since we'll be searching for the boy, we'll be on the lookout for Henson too." The ranger they hadn't yet met approached from behind Carter and held out his hand to each of them in turn. "Ranger Harley Feeney. Best tracker on Carter's team. I'd be the boss if he'd get with the program and retire."

Emma gripped his hand, noting the solidity of the grasp. He had his shirtsleeves rolled up. A tattoo of Smokey Bear warning of forest fires took up his entire muscular forearm. His long brown ponytail didn't scream authority, but she couldn't have dreamed up a man who looked more like a tracker. "Nice to meet you, Ranger Feeney." She glanced around the area. "Is it just us for the search?"

Feeney scoffed. "Of course not."

Emma turned in a slow circle. "Then where's everyone else?"

He grinned at her. "I should have said 'of course not…for now.'"

Emma wasn't in the mood for verbal games. "Then where are the others?"

"Back at the station. We're going to scout ahead while the others coordinate a more extensive search operation. Drones, dogs, full ground teams, the works. We're just the first wave. Call me Harley. 'Less you want to call me a curse word, but that's fine as long as you listen to me. Come on, you three new kids." Harley turned his back and headed to the SUV he'd been hovering near.

Before Emma could respond, District Ranger Carter spoke up. "He's prickly, but he's got a point about names. Let's cut the formalities. It'll make life easier if we think of one another as family."

The sentiment wasn't lost on Emma, and the looks on Leo's and Mia's faces told her they felt the same way.

"I can't argue with that logic, Ben." She held out a hand, and he shook it, doing the same with Leo and then Mia, exchanging names again with a smile.

Laurie Mason repeated the little ritual, nodding toward Harley, who was leaning halfway into the SUV and pulling out gear. "Don't let his attitude turn you off. He's the best we've got and knows the area. Last thing we need is an FBI agent going missing while trying to find some lost hikers."

"Not just lost hikers," Emma stressed. "There's a child in imminent danger somewhere in this area."

With a solemn nod, Laurie led Emma and the others, with Ben trailing behind, to where Harley was counting out rations and stowing them into packs. "Harley was part of the expedition that searched for the hikers after that foot discovery. It's to his credit that everyone in the search party got in and out safely."

"You done blowing hot air, Mason?" Harley hefted the three packs out of the SUV. "Because sunlight's wasting."

She put her hands up and backed away, laughing. "They're all yours, Harley. Me and Ben'll get our packs ready while you give the city folk their rations."

Emma turned back from Laurie just in time to have a heavy pack shoved into her hands. Beside her, Mia and Leo were weighed down with the same. Harley gestured with a finger winding in a circle. "Have a look. Get familiar with what's in there."

Mia knelt on the ground and began digging through her pack. Emma did the same. Leo muttered beside her, whistling in appreciation of the work that had already gone into preparing for the trip.

Picking through the pack, Emma found stores of water, rations of jerky, nuts, and granola bars, a blanket, a first aid kit, and a fire-starting kit, along with emergency flares. She also found basic cooking implements—most notably, a small metal cup for boiling water and a sharp knife. There was even an electric lantern.

Standing above them all, Harley adopted a pedantic tone as he gestured to the various packs in turn.

"Y'all have basic rations and water, supplies for starting a fire, and rudimentary first aid in the outer pockets of your packs. Inside is a change of clothes and blankets. The rest of the gear is split between you. Last has the cooking supplies, Ambrose the more extensive medical kit, and Logan extra dry clothing."

Mia lifted a pair of socks as if to lend credence to Harley's information.

"Carter's pack has the evidence-collection kit," Harley continued, "along with a second medical kit that more than covers the basics. Mason's carrying a four-person tent that we'll just have to squeeze into if we need to take cover overnight, along with extra rations for everyone. I have rope to tie snares or help us navigate any vertical terrain, plus some extra firepower. You're all carrying firearms, I assume."

Leo gaped at him. "We are, but is all this necessary?"

Emma zipped her pack back up, fighting off an uncomfortable flashback to the year her father enrolled her in a nature club. The pack had to weigh fifty pounds, at least. "How long are we planning on being out there?"

Harley laughed. "Asking those kinds of questions is your first mistake. Preparedness is *always necessary*, and you always want to prepare to be out longer than you expect. We done with the dumb questions now?"

Mia raised her hand, fighting an impish smile that still shined through. "Yes, sir. Sorry, sir. Can I ask you to call us by our first names? I'm Mia, in case you forgot, and these two bigmouths are Emma and Leo."

Leo coughed to hide a laugh, but Emma grinned, as did Harley. He crossed his arms, making Smokey Bear's raised hand disappear into his bicep. "Will do, Mia. I like you, by the way." He peered between Emma and Leo. "She can stay on my six, and I'll be glad to have her. You two, the jury's out on."

Searching for a response, Emma was jarred into one when Harley knelt in front of her and poked at her boot. "Excuse me?"

"Lift your foot. And your pants, if you don't mind."

Leo moved in beside her, a step closer. "Ranger—"

"Calm down, Leo. I need to check all your boots. Make sure you're fully equipped for this territory." He glanced up. "You want me to start with you? That make you feel better?"

Emma shook her head in wonder at how extensive this prep was but bent down and lifted the hem of her jeans obediently. "And I dressed in layers too. Do I meet approval?"

Harley ran his eyes up her body in a way that would've been creepy in a different situation, but somehow communicated a particular sort of education in this instance.

A memory bubbled up in Emma's mind of when Oren

had stood in her kitchen and regaled her and Mia with details of his hike through Great Falls Park. On the way back, he'd stopped by to surprise her with a spray of winter flowers, including lavender. Then his nature-loving stories of the trip had brought frozen paths, icy pools, bare trees, and slow rivers into her apartment.

He would've love coming out here.

Taking a breath, Emma centered herself the way Oren had taught her during yoga practice. She would appreciate the beauty of the wilderness he'd loved instead of spiraling over his absence. As Marigold had said, he was around, just behind the scenes.

Still crouched before her, Harley nodded when he'd finished his inspection. "Your flannel could be thicker, and your tank top could be sturdier. You're gonna get holes in it if you fall into trees. But the boots are good, and the jeans are thick. You pass. Should lose that FBI jacket, though. It won't breathe worth anything in those woods, and you're gonna get hot fast."

"No can do." Emma gave a critical eye to her official jacket, nonetheless. "The vests underneath our jackets stay on too. This is official business, and anyone we come up on out there needs to be able to identify us on sight."

The man muttered something about government red tape. "Fine, but consider how much extra water that might require you to drink."

She nodded, keeping her irritation at his superior tone beneath a straight face.

With Emma's inspection done, Harley moved on to Leo and Mia.

Leo's boots were pronounced more expensive than sturdy, a city boy's waste of money, but they'd do, and Harley seemed slightly impressed by his pocketknife, kept sharp, and the waterproof book of matches.

Mia's plaid overshirt was pronounced a hair too thick, but just fine for the day, as long as she didn't mind going down to her t-shirt and tying it around her waist.

"Now," he turned to the back of the SUV, gesturing them to gather around, "this map has all the spots marked just like that one in Payne's house. We're gonna start with this clearing right here, since that makes for the easiest trail start, and then move over here." He drew a line with his fingertip across the map. "Pay attention, all right? I don't want to repeat myself."

Emma did pay attention, listening as he outlined the route and following his finger as he detailed minor obstacles they'd pass and his reasoning for each decision. At the same time, nerves ate at her.

Leo had a calm set to him that suggested he was reassured by the man's confidence, and Mia positively glowed in the morning air. Without question, the two of them trusted Harley to get them in, get them out, and find what they needed to—if they could—in between.

And it wasn't that Emma didn't trust him.

Harley seemed more capable than she could've hoped for.

But right here, in the shadows of Buckskin Wilderness and on the heels of a surprisingly extensive gear check, she couldn't help feeling anxiety rise through her blood and warn her to be more careful than her colleagues. If this were a simple hiking trip, she'd have felt fine. Excited, even.

This little trip was a lot more than that, though. They would be in unfamiliar territory that seemed to swallow hikers at every opportunity. They'd also probably be dealing with a man in the fits of TBI-induced active psychosis, whose reason had likely scattered to the wind.

One way or another, the time for preparation had run out. Emma hefted her pack alongside Leo and Mia as Harley finished folding his map and tucked it into a pocket. He gave them a last once-over, doused them with bug spray, then locked his SUV and headed up the rise to the trailhead entry point.

It was time to find Will Payne and his father.

16

Emma followed Leo, who walked just behind Mia and kept to Harley's heels. Behind the four of them, Laurie and Ben brought up the tail of their procession. Within fifteen minutes of hiking a steady incline into the forest, Emma saw the wisdom in Laurie's short bob. Direct sunlight couldn't make it down so far as the forest floor and trail in most cases, but even this early in the morning, the humidity was a beast.

And bugs were only slightly deterred by the spray-down Harley had insisted on. Emma didn't last long before rolling down her long sleeves for a bit of extra protection. Ahead of her, Mia joked that the mosquitoes would drain her dry before they got to their first destination.

Soon after that, Harley came to a slow halt and pulled his map out again. As they gathered around, he circled the *X* closest to the edge of the forest. "This is the first destination, and it seems clear this isn't where Payne built his cabin. Let's take a water break and look around, just in case he was in the area recently, before we move on."

Nobody argued. The packs—loaded down with six quarts of water per person, MREs, and everything else Harley had packed for them—had gotten heavy fast. Emma hadn't ever lugged around this much weight on her back, and her shoulders had already begun complaining.

She rubbed one as she sipped water, taking the respite for what it was.

They conducted a sweep of the area. The three rangers, with Harley in the lead, identified game and wildlife tracks, but found no sign of human activity.

They packed up and got moving again.

Farther along the trail system, Leo began asking questions about the larger wilderness. The rangers more than proved their knowledge of its history. But the recital of lost hikers dating back into the mid-1900s made Emma feel no better about their current mission. By the time they'd crossed another *X* off the map, nerves had settled into her gut.

"What makes this wilderness so dangerous?" Emma sipped the water bottle she carried, slowing just a touch as Laurie sped up and began walking alongside her.

"There are different answers to that, but common thought in our office is that this terrain is deceptive." Laurie gestured through the trees to a slow-moving stream. "For instance, see that? Fresh water, right? Great! But it gets freezing cold, and hypothermia can set in if you step into it too late or too early in the season. You'd be surprised how little exposure it takes to debilitate the human body."

Harley called back from above. "And there's the depth! You don't realize how far into the wilderness you are based on elevation because the terrain isn't straight up or straight down. It meanders. Doesn't take much effort to get miles and miles into nowhere and not realize what you've done. If you're not carrying a compass or paying attention, you can be heading into nothing for days."

"There's also a cliff." Ben huffed behind her, his age

starting to show as they moved a touch faster. "Out near the middle of the territory. Easy to stumble onto it. Fall and break your neck or a leg. Or make the dumb mistake of going traipsing into some cave that's home to a mother bear."

"Bears?" Mia stumbled to a stop, whirling to stare behind her and making the whole procession stop.

Harley let out a guffaw. "Why do you think I'm carrying tranks in my pack?"

A flash of movement caught Emma's eye, drawing a quick gasp from her. She'd expected a bear, ridiculous as that was, but instead she saw the faintest of outlines…and a white-eyed ghost matching their pace several steps to her right. Too far off for the Other to chill her, but there nonetheless.

And then gone before she could think of some excuse to investigate.

The others seemed not to have noticed her reaction, as they had all continued moving while she stared at the ghost.

With a sigh, she refocused on her feet and the path ahead, putting on steam to reclaim her position in the marching order. She kept just far enough back from Harley that she had a good idea of the footing—just as she'd been instructed.

Her feet ached, though her hiking boots were good quality. On another day, she might've asked if they'd ache less if she carried less weight, just to make conversation, but today, she saved her breath. In the humidity and with her sore muscles, she didn't see much point in wasting effort on chitchat.

Leo joked about how if Vance had to miss a case, this was the one, and Mia agreed he'd have hated the hiking and the wilderness, joking in return that she had to enjoy the fresh air while she could.

Emma smiled at the banter but couldn't quite make herself engage. And it wasn't just the very physical weight dragging her down at this point. The image of Harley's map with those *X*s felt like a physical haunting in her chest…one that brought its own chill.

They were deep into the woods now.

Harley stopped, telling them to take a water break as he paced around the outskirts of the circle. Emma watched him, distracted by the tightness around his lips. Was he nervous for some reason now?

Far in the distance, she saw another ghost flickering past, but again, it was gone before Emma could decide whether to investigate or how to separate herself to do so.

Too bad you can't talk to Mia and Leo about these spirits, Emma girl. Bet the rangers would love that.

At the head of the group, Harley was muttering to himself as he looked back and forth along the trail, then down to his map and his compass.

"Everything okay there, Harley?" Ben stepped up beside him, peering down at the map in his hands. "We on track?"

"'Course, we are." Harley still stared at the map, though. "Come on. Let's move."

But soon it became a pattern that couldn't be ignored.

They'd walk for a five-minute stretch before Harley drew them to a halt and studied his map. Again. Sometimes, he'd pace to the back of the group.

Leo held a smile on his face and kept up the quiet banter with Mia until the third time they stopped within twenty minutes. Harley moved to confer with Ben some little ways away, voices lowered.

Laurie's face pinched, and she shifted the pack on her shoulders.

When Harley took off up the trail again, red-faced and with sweat on his brow, Emma traded quick glances with Leo, whose eyes had narrowed. Ben only shook his head and gestured them to keep on going.

But then they stopped again, and Harley pulled out his

map once more, and Emma decided she'd had about enough of being dragged along for the ride when something was clearly wrong. "Harley, you want to tell the rest of us what's going on?"

His eyes rose to meet hers. She expected him to ignore her or joke about them being a bunch of city slickers, but then he looked back down at his handy, ever-present map without answering.

"Is there something wrong with the Xs we marked?" Leo edged closer to him, pulling his pack from his shoulders and resting it against a nearby tree. "We didn't check the dates on that map in Payne's room. If it was out of date—"

Ben grunted behind him. "It wasn't any more out of date than any other. I looked at it."

Harley folded up the map, sighed, and met each of their gazes in turn. "The map I've got is the most up-to-date there is, except it's not."

Emma blinked at him, waiting for him to make sense, and then pressed. "It's not what?"

"Not up-to-date." Harley kicked one boot against a tree, shaking some leaves down. "But it's all we had, map-wise. The trails aren't matching up."

"What do you mean?" Emma wasn't sure she wanted an answer but had to ask.

He turned and stared off into the trees, then pointed. "You see that big line of boulders? According to the map, the trail we just followed should've brought us out to the right of that formation. But it's to our left instead."

Mia stepped forward, following Harley's gesture. "Maybe there's more than one trail."

Ben shook his head, frowning. "And you think someone moved the stream that should be coming up to cross the path too?"

Harley ignored them, bending down to dig into his pack.

He dug out a number of little devices, including two separate types of compasses. Then he stood up and glared around the circle of observers. "Compasses will be good enough, so don't panic. This is an annoyance, not an emergency. Now, stay put while I go up this hill and triangulate exactly where we are. Understood?"

Ben gave him a firm nod that looked more military than ranger-produced, maybe because of the hard set to Harley's jaw. Their guide stalked away into the trees.

"Nobody could've sabotaged people with compasses, right?" Emma glanced around the group, focusing on the rangers. "That would take, what, magnets?"

Laurie shook her head, watching Harley as he moved through the trees. "You'd have to have serious magnetic power."

"Which we don't." Emma sighed in relief. "Makes you wonder why everyone doesn't depend on compasses instead of maps, the way today's going."

"Ha." Ben raised one eyebrow and gestured around them. "Trails don't follow exact directions, Emma. They're not laid out in a grid like a city block. Using a compass and trail map at the same time is a little more complicated than you'd expect."

Taking the man at his word, Emma sipped her water while Harley moved around in the trees.

When he came back to them, he hefted his pack without a word, clearly having accomplished what he'd meant to. Harley huffed as he turned on his heel, red-faced with frustration. "You all follow behind me and stick close."

Without another word, he trudged off into the woods, leaving the trail. He headed toward the line of boulders he'd signaled as Leo grabbed up his pack and the rest of them hurried after. Emma moved ahead of the group, keeping to Harley's heels and watching the woods ahead of him.

Something felt off, and it wasn't just the nerves in her gut or the talk of bears. The trails they'd been following felt erratic.

When their guide reached the rocks, he trekked ten feet off to the right, shoving himself through branches so rough and thick that Emma had to keep a hand up to avoid being hit in the face as she followed him.

"Fucking hell!" He kicked at a pile of leaves, staring off into the trees. "You gotta be shitting me. Dammit!"

Emma froze when he started cursing and stayed put as the others came up around her. "That's a lot of expletives for a man who's got Smokey Bear tattooed on his arm."

He turned on her, huffing out a breath, and for a moment, she thought he might take a swing, but then he wilted. Leaning against a tree, he swiped one arm against his face and searched out the gaze of the lead ranger among their party. "Ben, I should've seen it sooner. Someone's been fucking with the trails up here."

Ben breathed out a whistle, and Emma followed behind him as Harley knelt among the leaves.

"Look here. Someone's pushed around debris to cover up this trail. See how the soil's been disturbed over there?"

Emma followed his finger off a few yards, and sure enough, a swampy area of ground looked abnormally clear of branches and leaves…which had been spread over the trail in front of them.

"They've covered up this part of the trail completely." Harley stood and gazed off into the trees in various directions. "I was here not long ago, right before the weather turned last October. No way did anything natural cause all this confusion. Some yahoo's been up here screwing with the trails on purpose. No wonder people are disappearing. They don't have a trustworthy map."

Emma remained quiet, and the other agents did the same,

as if by agreement. Laurie walked ahead, kicking leaves and branches off the apparent trail, then turned back to Harley. "It's gonna take a lot of work to put things to rights, but this isn't the time."

Ben sighed, shaking his head. "No, it's not. Least of all when we've got a ten-year-old boy lost up here with a man who may or may not be in his right mind."

Clearing his throat, Leo waited for the rangers to focus on him before he spoke. "I agree, but what does this mean, exactly? Are we lost? Or is there a way for us to keep going forward?"

Harley straightened, his lips set firm. "We go by landmarks. And the map may not be completely useless, Xs aside. Unless there's a whole gang of troublemakers aiming to destroy the trails up here, which I think we would've been aware of well before now." He swept his gaze over the treetops. "Now that we know the map isn't reliable, we can be on the lookout for problems. It'll just be slower going. First thing is to look for a vantage point to triangulate our location based on these landmarks and distance. Give me a minute."

Ben nodded in agreement, then glanced from agent to agent as Harley returned his focus to the tools he'd consulted earlier. "You three know more about Payne than anyone. You think he's so paranoid that he'd want people lost up here? What would the point be?"

"I don't know." Emma furrowed her brow, watching as Harley and Laurie worked in opposite directions, clearing some of the path while they'd stopped to reassess. "Lost people are just as liable to stumble on him and his son as anyone else."

"They'd be even more likely." Mia shook her head. "They'd be wandering around, looking for help, keeping an eye out for anyone who might know where they are. And there'd be no predicting where they are, so he couldn't avoid them."

Leo grunted his agreement, shifting his pack on his shoulders. "Mia's right. Payne could've just avoided building his cabin near the trail system to begin with. Something's not adding up."

Emma opened her mouth to say they'd just have to keep going, but the cold of the Other swept away her words.

Behind Ben, just a little way into the forest, another ghost had appeared. But this one was staggering toward her. The man was thin and blond. His shirt was torn open, and blood, shredded skin, and exposed muscle erupted from a rip across his chest and stomach. It was a mass of gore.

She swallowed down the bile that rose in her throat, watching his terror-stricken face and white-eyed gaze approach. He was clearly staring at her.

"I'm inside…he took me and put me on the inside."

The man choked on blood, which erupted out of him and sprayed out into the nothingness between them. Instinctively, Emma stepped back, and Leo's eyes narrowed on her as Ben raised an eyebrow in her direction.

"You okay?" Ben cocked his head. "We're gonna be fine, Emma, don't you worry."

She choked on a reply as the ghost came right up alongside Ben and swayed, more blood spitting out of his mouth and disappearing in the air.

"Yeah. Yeah. I'm okay," she finally managed. "Just, uh, thought I saw a bear."

Ben peered through the trees, then turned back to her with a sympathetic smile. "The shadows can play tricks on you out here."

Emma looked at Leo, her eyes wide. After a moment, he gave her a small nod. Harley had pulled out his map again, and Leo drew the older ranger over to it with a request that he show them some landmarks he and the other agents might keep an eye out for.

Emma only stared at the ghost spitting blood, trying to ignore the shine of his intestines that were leaking out of his body as he swayed, repeating his odd mantra.

"I'm on the inside. He took me and put me on the inside."

"Okay." Emma's whisper barely broke the air, and Mia stepped between her and the others, shielding her. "Okay. I get it."

This wasn't the time for conversation, but she'd gotten the ghost's message loud and clear. They had to find Steven Payne's cabin, because he'd pulled this man—and who knew who else—inside it and butchered him.

Her vision went slightly foggy, and a voice called her name from another direction. Feminine and seeking. The same voice as before, the one that had protected her from the menacing voice inside Payne's home. She searched beyond the bloody ghost in front of her, blocking out his mantra, but didn't see any other sign of ghostly visitors.

"Hey!" Harley's voice rang out through the woods, silencing the birds and cutting off the moan of Emma's name. "Everyone, over here. I found something. And watch your step!"

There wasn't time for Emma to search beyond the immediate area, let alone for ghosts, so she turned away. Harley wouldn't be hollering at them like that for nothing.

17

Harley bent in the middle of the newly cleared trail, holding one arm out at a right angle to stop anyone from stepping forward. Emma would've done the same, as her eyes were glued to dangerous-looking wire just a step ahead of them.

Razor wire, like what she'd have expected outside a prison, not a hiking trail, and from the intakes of breath around her, she guessed the others knew it too.

And that's blood on that wire. No question.

"Folks, we've gone from stupid yahoos mucking with trails to dangerous assholes with bloodthirsty intentions." He finished tugging a heavy-duty glove on. "This is a snare built for a human, no question. This razor wire's attached to the tree."

Ben stepped to the side, needlessly pointing to the spot where the wire had been anchored in by a bolt at the base of the tree trunk. The wire ran up into the branches.

Harley picked up the snare carefully, between two fingers, and held it up so they could see it more clearly. The loop of razor wire was twelve to fifteen inches in diameter, big enough for any one of them to have stepped into if luck wasn't on their side. "Way it works is, if someone steps in and keeps walking, their toe will scoop up the front of the wire, and it'll tighten around their ankle and dig in like a noose when it gets pulled. You can see the dried blood, since you've all got eyes."

Leo grunted in agreement. "It snared someone already."

Mia let out a breath. "Who'd do this?"

But Harley was still going. "This trap isn't done." He stood, holding the snare, and gestured for them to step back. "See how this wire runs up the trunk? Look where it runs to."

Emma followed the wire up into the branches, then two trees over to a bundle of sticks carefully set across the branches of a tree farther up the trail. Her heart thudded harder in her chest on seeing the big picture—the trap in its lethal totality—and she almost wanted to tell Harley to stop talking so she didn't have to hear the truth of it.

"This wire gets pulled taut by an ankle, which triggers the whole system and pulls those sticks out." He yanked on the wire.

Sure enough, the sticks tumbled away, releasing three large rocks that had been piled precariously on top of them. The whole mess fell directly onto the trail below, right where the trap was laid. Harley straightened, his mouth set in a grim line. "Somebody's trying to kill people out here. For what reason, I can only guess. We need to mark this trap and trail so we don't stumble across it coming out."

Ben cursed under his breath. "Whoever did this meant to deter people from coming into the area or kill them because they'd come too close to some illegal goings-on. I'm betting we'll find a drug operation at some point. Everyone, watch your step going forward. You see anything at all out of place, you freeze and you yell. Understood?"

Emma's gut spilled over with anxiety as she watched Harley cut apart the razor wire with a multi-tool he carried on his belt. He clipped out the section that had blood on it and stowed it in an evidence bag, which he secured in an outside pocket of his backpack.

He and Ben set about making marks on the nearest trees, cutting away the lowest branches they could reach to ensure they could identify their path again.

With that done and the trap fully disabled, Harley explained some of the snares they should watch out for too. "Trip wires can simply be used to knock someone down, or they can trigger something else, like we just saw."

Ben called for them to wait as they reached the fallen rocks and branches. He stepped up beside Harley to inspect the mess before giving the go-ahead to continue on.

"Other sorts of traps we need to look out for," Harley used a branch to edge some brambles to the side of the trail they'd been following, "are pits you could fall into, either with weapons inside them or just meant to make you break an ankle and trap you. And watch out for netting or snares that could be triggered to pull you up into the trees. You could be stuck out here yelling yourself hoarse for days if you don't have a knife to cut yourself free."

"But we have each other." Mia's step faltered as she passed by leaves that had drifted into the path. She stepped around them.

Laurie sipped from her water bottle as they moved forward. "Unfortunately, having people with you won't stop you from breaking your arm or getting knocked flat under rocks and branches."

Ben stepped up near Harley, inspecting the path ahead. "We'll move faster if I help you clear as we go." He stepped off the path and picked up a fallen branch, not unlike the one Harley was using to clear the trail.

He took a step back onto the path and turned to face Emma, holding up the branch he'd grabbed. "Find more like this one and do your own clearing, in case we miss anything." Ben stepped backward and toppled over, flailing his arms as he went down with a crash.

"Aaaahhh!" His scream of agony chilled Emma's blood.

Harley swung both his arms out to stop everyone. "Freeze! Nobody else move."

High-pitched whimpers bled up from Ben's throat. His breath was ragged and heavy.

Emma didn't dare move until Harley gave the okay, but Ben was clearly injured and badly.

Harley swept his branch forward, prodding at the area where Ben had tripped. He uncovered a wire strung between two young trees. Then he brushed the end of his branch against some kind of frame or construction that was half-buried in the ground beneath Ben.

"Oh, no. Fuck." Harley froze. "Leo, we need that first aid kit, and Laurie, try the satellite phone. Quick!"

Ben groaned. "Get me off this thing, Feeney. C'mon."

"Not yet. Not until we know what we're dealing with and we're ready to patch you up. We take those spikes out of you now, you could bleed out."

Ben had fallen onto a trap that had to be five or six feet across. Harley cleared the debris and leaf litter away from it, murmuring to himself as his work revealed a frame made of stout branches about six inches in diameter.

Coming up to stand beside him, Emma spied the wooden spikes that had been tied onto the frame in a grid pattern. Some still sat, waiting for prey. Others, presumably, had broken beneath Ben or impaled him.

Three spikes ran up through his legs, blood pooling around them. Two stretched through the outside of his thighs, and another had hit him just below the knee, while still another had spiked through his jeans and at least grazed his ankle. Blood trickled from above his boot, and Emma could see more collecting at the edges of his legs.

He went to speak, had to catch his breath, and then leaned his head back at an odd angle, his eyes closed. Emma expected he was about to pass out.

His words came in fits and starts, pained. "Lucky I had my pack. Saved my back. My ass and legs are pincushions. I'm not in good shape, Harley. Get me offa this damn thing."

Harley knelt by the trap. "Leo, where's that medical kit? Laurie, you got anyone yet?" Harley eyed her, waiting for her to nod.

She did and spoke into the phone. "They can send in a rescue chopper. I'll direct them to our location."

Silently, all of them moved into action.

Emma rushed to help Leo collect clean bandages and prepare for whatever treatment they could offer in the woods. Harley sank down beside Ben while Laurie stayed on the line with the rescue team.

"Pull me up," Ben moaned.

Harley clasped Ben's hand. Across from him, Emma and Leo hunkered down to apply pressure around the stakes. "I can't, man. Not until SAR gets here. I'm not risking you bleeding out here on the damn forest floor."

Ben drew in a shuddering breath, his forehead beading with sweat. Emma leaned in close to mutter in Leo's ear. "We should treat him for shock."

With a quick nod, Leo pulled out an emergency blanket from his pack and spread it over Ben. The ranger closed his eyes, but his breathing evened out as Harley kept talking to him in a low, calm voice.

Laurie finished her call and helped Emma and the others place bandages around each wound.

Ben coughed. "If you pull me up, I can manage to get back to the trailhead."

With a sharp slice of his hand, Harley rejected the idea. "Save it, old man. No way are you walking out of here. Search has to be called off for now."

Emma swallowed down a desire to stay silent, ready to plead that they needed to keep going, but Ben beat her to it. "Laurie can stay with me. You're gonna keep going and find that boy. And we'll get more help in these woods as soon as we can. They'll send drones up."

Mia had gone somewhat pale, but she nodded. Harley squeezed Ben's hand and grunted his agreement. "If it were an adult and not a child, I might disagree, but I can't."

Leo picked up where Harley left off. "I agree. We need to find Will Payne and his father and figure out who the hell's been booby-trapping these trails."

"Because it may or may not be Steven Payne," Emma added. "We can't jump to conclusions."

"I agree with y'all." Mia nodded again, some color returning to her cheeks. She and Emma lifted the bottom of the blanket to better patch bandages around the stakes impaling Ben's legs.

Once they were done, Harley moved to stand, but the injured ranger gripped his hand. "You keep your eyes more open than mine were, and you get these people back out of these woods safe. You can do that, can't you?"

Harley nodded and gave Ben's hand one last pat before he stood.

Working carefully to not disturb Ben's position, the group pulled what they could from his impaled backpack and redistributed the gear among their own bags. Leo placed his medical kit and rations into his own pack and grabbed an extra canteen from Ben's. That left the ranger with plenty to drink still. The coming rescue effort would ensure he and Laurie weren't at risk of dehydration.

When preparations were finished, Harley edged them

around the trap, moving first. He grabbed a few fallen branches and passed them around.

"Knock back any debris so the trap can't be missed once they pull Ben off." He knelt and pulled two stakes and small red flags from his pack. "Usually save these for trails in need of attention, so our volunteers can find them easily. Even with GPS, it's easy to get turned around out here. They'll have to do for warning signs for now."

Emma snipped the trip wire and coiled it up beside one of the red flags Harley had placed.

With the trap marked, Harley pulled his pack on and prepared to set out again. "Laurie, make sure you give the rescue team a heads-up on that, yeah?"

She nodded and raised a hand to acknowledge Harley's request.

He ushered the remaining members of their search party forward, and they set out with the sound of Ben's voice echoing in Emma's ears. The poor man kept cursing himself for being so stupid.

He hadn't been—Emma knew that—but she had to keep her focus forward. She trudged on with the others and, soon enough, they'd left the spike trap and its victim behind.

Leo walked abreast with Harley, the two of them searching out more traps. Behind them, Emma and Mia kept their own eyes peeled, trusting Harley's instincts and knowledge of the wilderness.

When the air went cold and thick with the Other, Emma almost bit out an angry demand to be left alone, but then she saw the ghost. He stood to the left of the path, directly ahead. It was the thin blond man again.

Now, though, his lips were held shut even as blood leaked from the jagged gash across his chest and stomach. He raised one hand and pointed at Leo.

Emma's mind froze for an instant, but then she lunged forward and grabbed Leo's elbow. "Stop!"

Both men and Mia froze. Leo's upraised foot hung poised above the forest floor, but he quietly pulled it back, releasing a heavy breath.

Ahead of them, the trail showed only dirt at first glance—no leaves or debris to cover traps—but the wire snare's shiny outline could just be glimpsed peeking through the dark dirt of the forest floor.

Another step and Leo would've stepped right into it and potentially been caught up, literally, in the moment that followed.

The air went warm again, their savior ghost disappearing, and Emma fought back a sudden wave of shocked but grateful tears.

Harley backed the three of them off and used another stick to follow the wire sideways. It ran up a tree trunk, disguised as a winding, leafy green vine. He shook his head as he triggered it from a few steps back, bringing down an avalanche of logs on the trail where he and Leo would've stepped forward a few seconds earlier.

Had it not been for the ghost, they'd have been down two more people and in even greater need of rescue.

Harley shook his head as he cut the wire and pocketed it in another evidence bag. "Let's get this one marked too. We have to be more careful going forward. A *lot* more careful."

18

"You see all that, son? Know it?"

The boy shook beside me but stayed quiet. I was ready to grab him, to plant my hand over his mouth and stuff that scream I could see brewing down his skinny throat before it was the undoing of us.

Over the hill ahead of us, we could just see the prone figure of a ranger, with another one crouching beside him. The woman had called for help—I'd heard her, though I wouldn't have expected a phone to work up here.

Hell, I heard them saving the damn day. Or so they thought.

But the others had gone deeper into our range.

And now the two remaining were quiet.

"You have to be careful of people like that. Okay?" I poked his shoulder, and he turned away. "You can't trust them to be...safe. Like friends. They're not friends.."

The words sometimes came easy to me, sometimes hard. And I was trying to practice—to make perfect, after all—but my boy rarely ever responded. Hard to have a conversation with only one person talking.

All he seemed to do was shiver like a deer.

He'll get better. He has to get better.

But it meant something that he stayed quiet—meant I could plot away.

I thought about moving up on the two rangers, the injured one and the woman, and killing them both. It wouldn't be hard. Not how I liked to catch people so I could connect with them. But they were in my woods.

Maybe I should've ambushed those other four before they took off. I could've had them down before they'd known what I was about. Or maybe not. They all had guns on their hips.

Even the two who'd stayed behind, the hurt one and the woman. They had guns too.

I hated to admit it, let alone with my son shaking beside me, but I couldn't go up against four people with guns and expect to come out okay.

Even if two of them were women. One of them would shoot me down while I took the others. I'd kill one, yes, maybe two, and then I'd be injured, at least.

And now that I had my boy out here with me, that was too much to risk.

Those four were still close enough to hear the other two shout if we attacked them. That meant we were better just watching. Waiting for a better time.

I backed up and pulled at the boy's shoulder. He got the hint and rose with me.

Moving quickly, I paced the trail the other four had taken. The boy shadowed me, and I reached back to hold him by the shoulder.

Pulling him along to match my pace. Keeping him by me.

I no longer worried that he'd call out. He might tremble and whimper, but he knew to keep his mouth shut. He'd proved that by now.

This was the time for us to be silent, and I was proud of the boy for understanding that. Knowing that. It showed he knew how to be aware, like I'd been at his age.

Just like I needed a good son to be.

We stopped at the trap they'd ruined. Somehow, one of the women had seen it. And they'd made a real mess of it too. I'd have to hide it better next time.

Moving carefully, I pulled a package of razor wire out of my pack and cut a long length of it. The boy eyed me and seemed to focus in on the blood that leaked from my fingers, but I brushed it on my pants and waved for his attention to remain on the wire. "Watch me. Okay?"

He trembled like a leaf in the wind but nodded. Good enough.

Point by point, I set a new trap, showing him each move. When it came time to reach into the trees, I sent him up.

"You climb. Take the wire up there and hang it on that broken branch."

I pointed to the one that I snapped off the last time I was in this area. Hanging the wire on it would hold the trap, but if the wire was pulled by someone tripping over it, the trap would be sprung.

He hesitated, and I barked in his ear, "Climb. Now, you go up." I pushed him at the tree, and he found the holds. He was small and couldn't reach all of them, so I had to push him up until he could grab the lowest branch and get into the tree.

I passed the wire up to him and showed him how to loop it over the broken branch. With my hands making a circle, I made the motion he needed to do, and he seemed to get it. He set the wire loop over the branch, and I smiled.

My son was learning. He would know more soon, and he would survive. Like me.

When the branches and the sticks were set—the wire ready to be hidden so that it could later be triggered—I helped him climb back down, holding my arms up to catch him in case he slipped.

He managed on his own, and I held out the snare loop for him to place. But he jumped to his feet and moved back, nearly off the trail.

Eyes wide…cautious and scared. Refusing.

Refusing to help me.

"Not okay to say no." My voice was gruff, but I was pleased the words came easy. I thrust the snare at him again. "This is the easy part. No climbing, just set it down." He took another step back, whimpering.

Dammit.

My stomach felt hollow, like I hadn't eaten in days. The boy was broken in some way. Refusing to do this simple thing? It wasn't right.

I'd hoped he wouldn't end up useless like my last son. Even though I knew that son would never be able to learn, I had dreamed he might.

Then I found Will and knew my first son was just practice. I practiced being a father on that dummy, to do better than my parents did for me.

Will impressed me, but for the first time, I thought we might be heading for trouble. Heading for the point when I'd have to give up on him, too, like my parents gave up on me.

Maybe if I showed him what happened to bad boys, he'd be good. Maybe then he'd learn the ways of the wild.

19

Emma breathed deeply, doing her best to channel Oren's calming words from her past with him into her present moment mindset.

It didn't remotely work.

Even stopping for a water break, their group all but vibrated with tension. They'd spent every step searching for traps and expecting the worst. Emma's shoulders ached from both the weight of her pack and stress now.

As a reminder of the danger, Leo had stopped Harley from all but tripping onto another spike trap like the one that felled Ben, and Harley himself had grabbed Mia's elbow just in time to stop her from stumbling into another wire snare.

Both traps were dismantled and marked, with low branches cut off around them so others could see the traps and they could find the trail on their way out.

If there were just two of us watching these paths, we'd be doomed, Emma girl. It's taking all four of us to sniff out the danger, never mind searching for signs of Will or his father.

No ghosts had appeared since the one that warned her in

time to save Leo from that trap. But in the quiet of the forest, Emma guessed it was only a matter of time. She wanted to call herself paranoid and dismiss the expectation, but that ghost who'd helped her had been there for a reason.

And it hadn't just been to show off the fact that he'd been gutted like a buck during hunting season.

Someone, or something from the Other, is keeping tabs on you.

She wanted to believe it was Oren's work, from behind the barrier between life and the Other. He was looking out for her—he had to be—but it wasn't Oren she was running into, so…

"Everyone ready?" Harley glanced around their group, focusing in on Mia as she struggled to heft her pack from the ground again. "You good to go?"

She scowled at him and made a show of standing straight. "Ready to feel like we're risking our lives with each step, you mean?"

Harley sighed. "I meant the pack, but I get it. Y'all are holding up better than I expected."

The man had blamed himself repeatedly for allowing Ben to fall onto that trap. Tenser even than the forest full of booby traps called for.

Emma stowed away her water. "We're all on edge, but we're okay. We've all dealt with harrowing situations before." She kept her voice low and even. "And you need to stop feeling badly about not seeing every trap first. This has to be a group effort."

Harley opened his mouth to argue, but Leo waved him off. "You're a forest ranger, Harley, not an Army Ranger. Nobody trained you, or us, to be walking through a forest and searching out deadly traps at every step."

Finally, the man nodded and turned back to the path they'd been following toward the next destination. "I'll lead."

Emma moved in right behind him, eyes focused on the

shadows, leaves, and every pile of dirt that looked even slightly suspicious. It had been a good twenty minutes of hiking since they'd come across a trap, but that somehow made the situation worse.

Her gaze caught on a log that had fallen partially into the path, but Harley had seen it too.

He crouched carefully beside it, leaned forward, and examined it as best he could from all angles. When he stood and breathed out, then kicked it off the path, Mia released a loud sigh.

She glanced at Emma. "I know the boogeyman's not about to climb out of the dirt or from inside a log, but it kinda feels like it."

"Hey!" Leo pointed off the trail, northeast of where they'd been heading. "That look like a building to anyone else?"

Emma squinted into the murkiness of the forest, and Harley had agreed with Leo by the time she finally spotted a tiny building that blended into the trees and greenery. "Is that our next destination?"

Harley had the map out again, staring at it. "It's close enough to the next *X*. We can't get all the way to it via this path, but let's stick to the cleared trail for as long as we can. We'll go through the brush only when we have to."

With that said, he tucked away the map and led the way along the hiking path they'd been following for the last hour. Emma fought the urge to hurry him on and took out her angst on a mosquito buzzing too close to her cheek for comfort.

The slap she gave herself made Mia's head jerk toward her, and Emma flushed and showed the insect's bloody guts on her palm. "Sorry."

"We'll do another round of bug repellent and get some food in our systems at this cabin up ahead, whatever we find." Harley came to a stop on the trail, orienting himself toward the cabin that had now become a clearer shape within the trees. "I'm not gonna go in a straight line here. Follow me, and keep your eyes peeled."

Emma cringed with every step Harley took toward the cabin, her eyes on his calves and boots and the two square feet directly ahead of him. She ignored the ache in her shoulders and back to focus. Losing their remaining guide to a trap would be bad enough, but the idea of calling off the search to render necessary care was its own form of torture.

When Harley whistled ahead of her, coming to a stop in a small clearing, Emma finally brought her focus up to the cabin.

The structure could barely be called a cabin. Just from first glance, she could tell its dimensions were probably the equivalent of her own bedroom, if that.

Leo trudged forward, walking slowly enough to take care with each step. "This isn't anything Steven built this year. Thing's been here for decades."

Harley huffed, following him over to a rough opening in a wall, but one that no glass-encased window had ever been installed in.

Emma paced around the small building and bent forward to examine an abandoned wasp nest near another window. Inside, beyond the remains of the nest, she saw only shadows and rotted wood.

An acrid stink wafted from somewhere nearby, but she couldn't determine the source or even if it was inside or outside the structure. Nothing she could see inside seemed to be causing the smell, though.

Moving around to the opposite side of the cabin, she found a rudimentary firepit, set just far enough away from the building to be safe. A small puddle of water lay still in its center, dampening old kindling.

The back wall of the cabin had a door in it but no

windows or other rough openings. Beside the firepit, a maroon sleeping bag lay worn and crumpled in the dirt. Though tattered and well past its use-by date, the bag still offered some sign of the modern world.

Mia stepped forward and prodded it with a stick. "You don't think there are any snakes in this thing, do you?"

"Not likely." Harley stepped up from behind Emma, frowning down at it. "Timber rattlesnakes are still hibernating this time of year, even with the warmer weather we've been getting. Copperheads could be out by now, but you just need to watch where you're stepping to avoid them. We're already doing that, so I'm not worried."

Mia blinked at him. "I feel *so* much better, Harley, thanks."

Emma moved up to the side of the sleeping bag and ran her own walking stick along the lumpy fabric. No trap sprang, and no snake slithered out. She prodded the bag, using her stick to flip it open, and revealed only dirt and leaf litter mounded up and filling the inside. But something heavy seemed to be tucked into the very bottom.

"Nothing inside the cabin as far as I can tell." Leo walked up to the other side of the sleeping bag. "Just bad wood, signs of raccoons, and the most disgusting mold I've ever seen. Nobody's lived in there lately, if ever. There's a door to some little side room that's grown over with ivy and rot, but I didn't try it. Smell's terrible."

Glancing up at him, Emma wondered for a moment about the back door into that structure, but now wasn't the time. The sleeping bag, at least, wasn't covered with rot.

Prodding the zipper down, Emma fought with it for a second, then gave up. She used her stick to lift the upper portion of the bag and confirm no copperheads were lurking underneath. "We can cut it open to see what's in the base, or we can just turn it upside down."

In answer, Leo bent and gripped the bottom of the bag,

pulled it a foot back from Emma, and then brought it up. A lumpy object tumbled through and thudded to the ground at Emma's feet.

An ancient bank box with only one remaining hinge and rusted latches tumbled out.

Mia took a quick picture of the rusty object as Emma pulled gloves on before attempting to pop the latches with her multi-tool.

Inside, a collection of dusty rodent skulls stared up at Emma, as if daring her to retreat. Mia groaned and backed off, but Harley bent beside her. He prodded them with his finger. "Mostly mice and a bird skull."

Emma scanned the little collection, and her attention caught on something beneath it. She angled the box up, letting the skulls slide to one side. She reached past them to pluck up the photo that had lain beneath them, hidden by their macabre presence.

She set the box down and stood with the picture, heart pounding faster. The photograph was old and weathered, displaying a man and woman standing in front of a small house. The man's smile shined with gray teeth—an effect Emma didn't think she could blame on the age of the paper—and the woman beside him had dark eyes that appeared flat and soulless. Emma didn't know how else to describe them.

Harley whistled again, glancing over her shoulder. "Talk about a blast from the past."

"Who are they?"

The ranger hesitated a moment. He wiped a hand across his mouth. "The Grundys. The mister and his missus, Alan and Denise."

Emma flipped the photo over, trying to tell herself that the chill she got from looking at the run-down couple came only from her imagination. On the back of the photo, though, a trailing bloody fingerprint did nothing to dispel her anxiety. Beside the bloody print, in what looked like green crayon, were written the words *Momy* and *Dady*.

Mia grunted. "Not parents I'd want. Talk about creepy." She took off toward the cabin, likely to investigate that mystery door.

Despite agreeing with her, Emma held her tongue. It felt too much like tempting fate to comment, and she did *not* want to meet these two individuals as ghosts if they happened to be dead and wandering any more than she did if they were living and killing.

Leo leaned closer and sniffed the blood, but then shook his head. "No scent. Old as can be." He glanced to Harley. "You know these two, so care to fill us in?"

Still wide-eyed, Harley nodded with a pinch-lipped frown. "They lived in the county up until maybe ten years ago, just outside the forest line in a rural neighborhood. They were found dead in what looked like a murder-suicide. One of the neighbors saw the door left open one day, walked in, and found the bodies. Animals had already gotten in and eaten up what they wanted. Won't ever forget that scene."

Emma tried to soften her heart toward the man and the woman in the photo, but like Mia, she still felt unnerved by them. That man's gray smile and the woman's hard eyes gave an impression of darkness, no matter how hard she tried.

She pointed to the rough writing on the back beside the bloody print. "This would suggest there was a child. Do you remember if they had a son or daughter?"

Harley's brow wrinkled, his gaze shifting to the side. "Wasn't ever talk of one that I remember, and it seems like there would've been, considering…"

Leo dropped down beside the sleeping bag and peered inside, making sure they hadn't left any clues unturned. Determining it was empty, he simply nodded at the run-down shack. "Someone was living here. Maybe not recently, but the mold inside was growing on old packages of food, and this sleeping bag wasn't dragged here by a bear. If they didn't have a child and it wasn't them—"

"Hey," Emma shifted, thinking back to her meeting with the fortune teller, "didn't Esther say that Steven was fiercely private about his upbringing and his family? What if—"

"*Shit!*" Mia stumbled back from that strange, closed door at the back of the structure. When she turned to face them again, her expression had gone slack. "I thought I smelled something." All I did was shake the knob a little and the worst stench shot out to greet me. It's not even open yet."

Leo and Emma hustled her way, Harley hanging back. Within a foot of the door, though, Emma caught the stench.

Rotting flesh.

"It's coming from inside." She slid the photo into an evidence bag and handed it off to Harley, who'd suddenly appeared at her side. He bagged it as she pulled her gun, while Leo put one gloved hand on the rusted door handle.

He froze there, as if preparing himself, and Emma shivered. The cold of the Other encased her, strong enough to reach Leo and force him to pause.

Ghosts glimmered into view from all angles. All of them staring at the door on the shack.

20

Instead of opening the door, Leo felt around the doorknob, searching for traps, and Harley got down on his hands and knees to add his eyes to the effort.

He stood up again, swatting away flies. "Smell's stronger down there, but I don't see any wires."

Bugs, or maybe rodents, could be heard within the shack, now that Emma knew to block out the forest's natural sounds and listen for them. Buzzing seemed to echo out from under the door along with the odor, demanding witnesses to whatever they'd been feeding on.

Steady, Emma girl. You'd rather have this than a man swinging a machete at you, right?

She bent to peer into the cracks of the door, blocking out the presence of the ghosts surrounding them. She didn't see a thing, though.

The ghosts, on the other hand, were undeniably visible and demanding her attention.

Many of them were missing limbs, and all of them were bloody.

A man without his left arm and with a hole where his

heart should've been stood peering over Mia's shoulder. Off to his side, a woman whose leg looked to have been sawed off just below her pelvis stood with her arms crossed, blood dripping from slashed forearms and a hole in her jaw.

The worst, though, was a man whose intestines leaked out of his gut, bobbing against the ground as if trailing for fish or some rodent that might be interested in the ends. He swayed where he stood, blood dripping from his mouth and coating his long, gray beard.

Tattoos on his bare forearm showed a bald eagle with an American flag flying over the Vietnam flag, with the year 1968 printed in big block letters below. She guessed that meant he'd fought in Vietnam, but in the end, he'd arguably met just as bad an end here as he could've found there.

Emma didn't recognize a single ghost or see the one that had warned her earlier, which didn't particularly make her feel any better.

Gun raised in one hand and a flashlight in the other, she nodded at Leo, confirmed he was ready, and pointed her light at the door. The scent of rotting flesh hung in the air, and her gut turned at the thought of what they'd find. "On three?"

"Your count."

She began counting up, and he pulled as she reached "three."

The door yawned open, and the stench hit them like a tidal wave.

Sickeningly pungent, the sweetness of dead flesh and methane washed over them, removing any hint of pine the forest offered. Mia and Harley both stumbled back, hands to mouths, gagging. Emma clenched her lips shut alongside Leo, willing herself not to breathe even as he choked on the air beside her.

Three seconds, Emma girl. Three seconds to view what's inside, and then you turn away and breathe.

Fighting the urge to vomit, she stole two steps forward and sent the beam of her flashlight into the shack. The forceful smells of sour blood and bodily gases long held inside were as dense as a brick wall and made her eyes water. Harley gagged out something about methane and the stench being normal behind her.

Bones littered the floor like driftwood at the beach. Meanwhile, arms and legs—thighs, mostly—hung from the ceiling, drying. One leg had fallen to the stained wooden floor. Emma's flashlight beam hit it, and in the tattered and torn meat at one end, she swore she saw bite marks.

Two old freezers sat against one wall, both open and showing stacks of hacked-apart arms and torsos. A small, fist-sized lump of rotten meat, maybe a human heart, sat alongside a stretch of black mold that covered one wall and added to the stench.

That was at least thirty seconds without oxygen, and it would have to do.

Emma stumbled backward, joining Leo a good dozen feet from the shack. She turned away from it, bent forward, hands on knees, and breathed in some fresher, colder air. Her whole body was sticky with disgust, the smell of rotting flesh clinging to every breath she took. Bile rose up her throat, and she held one forearm to her face, willing it back.

The sound of sobbing brought her gaze up, and she saw a nearby ghost crying tears that dripped down her chin alongside blood that poured from between her lips. Beyond her, Harley was fighting back sobs of his own, and Emma had to look away from both the living and the dead temporarily.

Mia lost the battle with her own stomach and vomited in the woods, some feet back from where Emma and Leo remained bent over. Emma thought she should tell her to be careful of traps but didn't think she could speak without getting sick herself.

The cold had grown worse, and the ghosts all seemed to stand where they'd been before. When Emma's name suddenly echoed out over the little clearing, her blood chilled beyond the level it had dipped to with the horror inside the body shack. She glanced around, trying to appear casual, but her name kept echoing, and none of the ghosts seemed to be the source.

"This is worse than *The Texas Chainsaw Massacre*." Harley coughed, facing the woods as he sat down on his pack and rested his forehead in one hand. "I sure wish some Hollywood director would tell us he was playing a prank."

Emma finally stood up straight, though she had to keep fighting back against her gut's desire to evacuate its contents.

Beside her, Leo gagged as he stood, but met her eyes and nodded. "Thinking the same thing here. Whoever we're hunting is fully insane."

Emma fought to ignore the ghostly whispering of her name as she looked back to the shack's dark entrance. "Steven Payne was, by all accounts, a functioning member of society a year ago. You think this could be his doing?"

Mia walked over to them, jerkily, and with one hand tight to her stomach. "You think he was operating out of this place, doing…this? While building a cabin somewhere else?"

Harley choked on the air as he stood up. "'Scuse me. I'll be back." He stumbled back around the cabin, cursing, and they heard him vomiting moments later.

Emma turned her back on the cabin again, willing the forest to offer more fresh air. And then the words from earlier that morning, from the blond ghost, came rushing back to her.

"I'm inside. He took me, and he put me on the inside."

Her body went cold with realization, and she fought down another wave of bile that threatened to come up as she gagged against her hand. "That's what he meant." The whisper was guttural, but Leo heard her and raised his eyebrow.

"Emma? Everything okay?"

She looked around for Harley and saw he hadn't come back yet. "A ghost, earlier today, said something I didn't understand, but I think it makes sense now."

Mia wiped a hand across her mouth. "What makes sense?"

Wishing she was wrong, but remembering the bite marks she'd seen, Emma told them about the blond ghost. "I thought we were looking for a place like that," she gestured at the grisly shack behind them, "but this is a meat locker. A storage facility for someone who…"

Leo finished the thought for her. "For a cannibal. Whether he's Steven Payne or not…there are a whole lot more victims than we realized, and the killer has been at this for a long time."

"This can't be something the Grundys did." Emma pushed her shaking hand through her hair. "Harley said they've been dead for a decade, so it has to be whoever's setting the traps now. And Steven Payne is our prime suspect."

Though she was ready to continue, the cold of the Other had suddenly become harder on her skin. She shivered, violently, and backed off a step from the shack and the ghosts.

By the pursing of his mouth, she saw that Leo had taken note but couldn't discuss that with him now.

Moving away from the ghosts made no difference, though. They swarmed closer, bloody and moaning and with their white eyes narrowed in on her. They were uttering words now, but she couldn't make them out.

Her name was getting louder, however. Emma looked to

her friends, feeling panic rise up her throat with the bile, but a fog descended between them and her, and the Other closed in around her. On all sides.

She spun in a circle fast, looking for an avenue of escape, but a ghost with a bloody beard blocked her path. She turned again, but the man with his chest torn open and one arm missing was there in front of her, moaning her name as blood drained from a wound in his forehead.

Her vision went foggier, goose bumps rising on every inch of her skin, and she felt herself swaying on her feet, struggling to breathe in the cold air and keep herself centered like Oren would've told her to.

Behind her, Leo's voice rose with panic, but she was already losing consciousness, falling back, and she didn't even know why.

The world went black around her, icy air smothering her.

21

Monique had been waiting for this moment all night and half the day. Her body was tight from stress and contact with the Other, purified with spells. She'd barely eaten or had anything but water for nourishment, all because she'd been cleansing to work up to this very instant.

A chance to speak to Emma Last. To fulfill her duty to her.

So many times, she'd gotten *this close* to being able to reach Emma, only to fail at the last moment. On a few occasions, she'd been near enough to see an image of Emma's face, and when she'd called out to her, it even seemed like Emma was going to respond.

Now Monique could see Emma with perfect clarity, which had to mean the young woman was surrounded by ghosts. But where was she?

Monique focused beyond Emma, trying to see anything other than her and flashes of fog that signaled a pack of ghosts. For the most part, she saw only trees. Endless trees. She shifted, trying for a different angle, and finally glimpsed a sort of dilapidated shack. Other people, too, wearing FBI vests and jackets…who appeared to be horrified by something in their vicinity.

Swallowing down the nerves that had begun running through her, Monique allowed herself to take in more of the situation, and she focused in on the ghosts. One after another, they all bore signs of mutilation. Bloody and eviscerated and—

Don't look. Stop looking at the ghosts, Monique. Focus on Emma! She's the reason you're here.

Simply put, she *had* to get Emma's attention, and this was the time to do it.

Monique breathed in and began calling her name.

"Emma. Emma! Emma Marie Last, hear me, Emma!"

The agent's eyes widened in reaction, and Monique willed herself to remain calm and centered. This bond needed her focus. She called out again, louder now, and could tell from Emma's surprised expression that she was getting through.

Vision clearing further, Monique watched as Emma closed her eyes. She called out again, and a new warmth came into the air, breaking through the film of the Other.

Emma's presence. I'm doing it!

Monique was just about to call out again when icy air swallowed Emma's heat, beginning at her toes and then encasing her within an instant. Unable to fight it or consider what threshold she'd crossed, Monique closed her eyes and gave herself over to the arms of the Other.

22

Emma opened her eyes to thick, lush trees rising above her and the soft cushioning of soil beneath her. For a moment, she expected to see Leo's and Mia's faces hovering over her.

Instead, she breathed in the scents of herbs and incense.

Better than rotting flesh, Emma girl.

She inhaled the freshness, and the familiarity of the wild space came to her. This wasn't the Buckskin Wilderness, but the woods surrounding her hometown.

"Salem." She swallowed and pushed herself up to her elbows, welcoming the ability to breathe in deeply without gagging. Her body was light, though…weightless. She glanced down as she sat up fully and realized she'd become translucent.

Panic overwhelmed her. She looked just like the missing body parts of the ghosts she'd seen outside the murder shack.

But she felt healthy. And her senses worked well enough. And she had all her parts.

She scanned her surroundings, and her gaze locked onto a woman standing before her. Dressed in a long, filmy blue skirt that fell around her in layers and a black cotton top with ruched shoulders and a scoop neck, the woman radiated calm. A bouquet of herbs was gripped in her hands, and she wore the tiniest of thin-lipped smiles. Long, grayish-brown hair set off her ice-blue eyes.

Emma's breath stopped. "You're one of my mom's old friends."

"I am, yes. Gina and I were very close."

"Which one? I mean, who…what's your name? I have a picture of you with my mom and someone else."

"My name is Monique Varley."

Something wove into Emma's periphery through the trees on her right, another person's presence maybe, or just another ghost.

She focused on the woman ahead of her. The picture of her mother and her friends had three sets of initials on the back.

GC, MV, and CF. I didn't mention the initials, and she said her name was Monique Varley. Too close to be coincidence.

That put an end to the questions Emma had about one set of initials, but she wasn't convinced she could trust this woman. She'd summoned Emma to a meeting within the Other, but for what reason?

Emma opened her mouth to ask Monique for answers when a wave of anger flooded from between the trees. Tendrils of mist and scattered leaves hit Emma, nearly pushing her to the ground with their strength.

Monique clutched her bouquet of herbs and flinched backward as another wave of emotion—hatred, now—speared the air between them.

A shadow of a ghost was pulled along behind it, wavering in the air. Emma caught just a glimpse of a scowl directed at the air to her side. She searched the misty area for Monique and found her standing stock-still beside a tree.

She held a finger to her lips. "These ghosts are searching

for us, and they're accompanied by one who wishes you harm. Don't speak to any of them. Do not meet their eyes."

A nearly translucent woman in green chiffon stumbled between them, swirls of anger and rage radiating from her. Emma sidestepped the cloud of anger, biting her lip as the ghost moved between her and Monique.

Gradually, the ghostly woman in green faded back into the trees and disappeared.

Across from Emma, her mother's friend relaxed.

The woman was shorter than her, maybe five-five, and Emma got the sense that she was taking in every single detail of Emma's existence, returning the examination Emma couldn't help but engage in.

"I can't maintain our presence together for long. This bond. But I do need to speak with you."

Emma's tongue twisted in her mouth, wanting to disagree. As desperate as she was to know what the woman wanted with her, this really wasn't the time. "I'm needed—"

The woman raised one hand, shaking her head while wafting the herbs forward and back around them. "This won't take long. You only need to know that I *am* your mother's friend. I placed a protective spell on you. Long ago. That spell is allowing us to speak like this. We have an enemy who's trying to break our bond. You just saw her, and she may return at any moment."

A man's ghost sprang between them, a cloud of rage spiking out from all around his form. Emma's skin prickled where the ghost had come close to her, and she fell backward. Could the ghosts hurt her?

Monique waved at her, eyes flashing. "I'd hoped that we'd never need the spell, but we do."

Emma swallowed, bringing herself back to the moment. "Why do we need it? What's this about?"

More ghosts filled in gaps between the trees. Emotions

flared out in angry, hateful blasts that seemed to be targeted at Emma.

Her mom's old friend sidestepped a ghost that swam near to her, and Emma got the message loud and clear—they couldn't allow these ghosts to touch them.

The woman waved her bundle of herbs and met Emma's eyes again.

"Your mother and I were friends with another woman. She's…our other, former friend who is not to be trusted." Monique grimaced, taking a fast step back to avoid a trio of ghosts pushing between them.

Howls erupted in the distance, bringing goose bumps up all along Emma's arms again.

"The other woman in the picture? What's her name? Who is she?"

"I cannot speak her name."

Emma breathed in and out, grounding herself in Monique's confidence as more ghosts came through the trees.

When Monique spoke again, her voice was distant, muffled, as if they were talking on an old long-distance phone line. "She's planning something big. Terrible. She may be close to breaking the protective spell I placed." She glanced around, then shouted the rest of her message, flinching away from ghosts as she did. "She may be lusting after far more power than I realized, and there isn't time for us to plan now. I need to see you in person. I need you to come back to Salem."

Emma's heart beat faster even as she struggled to hear through the fog around them. The air had gone cooler and grown heavier, the Other encroaching on the conversation and weighing her down. Ghosts spun between them, and Emma nearly had to dance to avoid them. She could feel herself on the edge of being pulled back to Virginia.

"I've been feeling an urge to come back to Salem. As soon as I can—"

"Yes. Do it. Listen to me." Monique stepped closer, her hands moving fast as she began an intricate waving of the herbs, which Emma was just realizing had the nuance of a pattern. "Outside Salem, come to my home, in the wilderness preserve east of the city."

Emma struggled to hear her over the howling as she dodged another ghost's dagger of anger.

Monique held firm, standing upright as ghosts wove around them both. When the bulk of the angry spirits had passed by, Monique continued her instructions. "Drive as far as the road allows. Park at the gate and walk in. Feel for my influence through the Other, and you'll find me."

Another flood of ghosts swam toward them, and Emma dodged sideways, eyes on her mother's friend. Trying to find the truth. The directions were simple enough—she could remember them—but should she?

She put my life in danger, bringing me here like this.

Emma fell backward, into the soil of the forest, and found the bloody woods of Virginia materializing around her once more as a wolf's howl split the fog that had descended around her.

23

Leo sat on his pack across from Mia, who continued rubbing water over Emma's brow. They'd both been startled when her eyes clouded over and she began mumbling and staggering around like a puppet at the end of someone's strings.

Her arms and legs jerked this way and that, until finally, she'd fallen and he caught her before she hit her head. What had, at first, felt like an *easy enough to explain* fainting episode from all the gore and trauma they'd uncovered seemed more worrisome now.

People wake up from normal fainting spells immediately.

"What's it been? Five minutes?" He waited for Mia to answer, but her lips tightened instead.

Somewhere on the other side of the cabin, Harley paced through the brush and muttered to himself as he tried to get a phone signal, but that wasn't Leo's first concern. His heart beat with what was closer to panic than he'd have liked to admit, and Emma still lay unconscious between them. If she didn't wake up, what exactly were they supposed to do? She was breathing fine, her pulse was fine—well, slow, but within the normal range.

Did he just assume she was fine and work together with Mia to get her out of the forest? Or assume that moving her could injure her and split their already shrunken group between a desperate trek for help and guarding her?

Shit. We're screwed either way.

Leo reached into the inside pocket of his jacket, searching for the gum he had tucked there. Cinnamon wasn't exactly a smelling salt, but it might do the trick.

"It's not like she hasn't walked into scenes of dismemberment or decapitation before. Other gruesome stuff." He unwrapped a piece of gum and waved it beneath Emma's nose. "And she didn't faint right away then."

Mia held her hand on Emma's brow.

"Her eyes didn't go all milky white either, so—"

Emma's eyes snapped open, wide and aware. Her whole body spasmed, and the piece of gum flew right out of Leo's hand as he jumped in surprise along with her.

As Mia breathed out the loudest sigh he'd ever heard, he sat back on his heels, swiping the nervous sweat from his forehead. "Talk about giving us a dang scare. You okay?"

She pushed herself up. "What happened? How long was I out?"

"Um…maybe five minutes. Your eyes were…well, they're normal now. But they weren't at first, and then you kinda fainted."

Mia reached for her. "We tried to talk to you, because you were saying something. We just couldn't understand a word of it, and your eyes…"

Something in Emma's face shifted, like she was suddenly very far away in her mind, and Leo was ready to jump forward and catch her in case she fainted again. "Emma?"

"I'm fine. I'm okay." She looked at him, then at Mia. "I was in the Other. I'll explain later."

Mia put a hand on Emma's arm. "Was Ned there?"

"No, it wasn't Ned." Emma glanced from Mia to Leo. "It was a woman named Monique, but she wasn't a ghost…I think she's one of my mom's friends. But we'll talk later. We've kind of got a cannibal psycho on the loose. Unless you two caught him while I was out?"

Leo shoved himself to his feet with a grunt, stretching his shoulders and releasing some of the tension built up over the last few minutes. "Maybe you're that good, Emma, but I'm not. I need more than five minutes when there's an empty crime scene and no tech to be had. An hour, at least."

With an eye roll at Leo, Mia gripped Emma's forearm and helped pull her upright. "Harley's been trying for a cell signal, but he's got nothing so far. Says it's normal, but that doesn't help us."

Emma nodded, but her gaze remained unfocused. She shivered, visibly, and Leo dipped his attention to where she'd earlier rolled up her jacket sleeves. Her bare skin was goose-pimpled with cold.

She let out a heavy breath. "There are ghosts around here. They were here before I fainted, and they're here now. The same one who helped me stop Leo from walking into that trap earlier—"

"I should've known." He shook his head. "Sorry. Didn't mean to cut you off."

She offered a thin-lipped smile. "This is the same ghost who said earlier that, uh, he'd been 'put on the inside.' I don't know whether the killer is Payne, but either way, it seems like the couple in that picture must have had a child. I don't know what else that writing could mean." Emma took out the photo.

Mia frowned. "Could be just a child who *wants* parents."

But then she took another look at the picture. "No, never mind. Scratch that. You wouldn't look at that picture and want *those* parents."

Emma sighed, shoulders slumped. "But we all agree these people are somehow involved. Victims, parents, relatives, or friends of some sort…what's happening in these woods is directly related to them, one way or another."

When they circled the little shack, she waved for Harley's attention. The man's ponytail had come loose, and he'd worried it into a matted mess strung over his shoulder. Other than that, and his slightly widened eyes, the ranger looked ready to keep up their search. At least one thing was going right.

"Harley, I think we need to get out of the woods." Emma pointed to his phone. "Unless you've had luck with that thing."

He stuffed it into a pocket. "Laurie had the satellite phone. No joy with this thing, and I agree. We need more than the four of us, with traps and body parts jumping up in every corner of this damn forest."

Leo held up the photo before Harley could grab his pack. "What else can you tell us about them?"

"The Grundys?" The ranger swallowed visibly, and Leo wondered if it was due to the question or the odor of rot in the air. "Not much to say. They kept to themselves. I don't know what they did for work, but they owned a house. Man might've driven a truck. He spent a lot of time in these woods hunting game. We never got complaints about them at the station."

Mia cocked her head, glancing at the picture and then back to Harley. "Do you know of any friends of theirs who still live in town? Anyone who'd know for sure what they did in the woods or if they had a kid?"

The ranger shifted on his feet, eyeing his pack like he was

anxious to get going. "They didn't have friends that I know of. Never saw anything but one vehicle in their driveway either. As for a kid…" His face tightened. "I don't know. But if it's all the same to you three, I think it's time we get gone. Can these questions wait?"

Leo shifted his pack on his shoulders, trying not to picture the image of those torn-up body parts inside the shack actually jumping up at them. Luckily, if he could call any part of this case lucky, there had been no children's limbs or bones in the mix.

He'd taken some photos while Emma was passed out, leaving Mia to watch over her. The thought of looking at those images turned his stomach again, and he made a mental note to include a content warning on any message he sent to Jacinda.

Assuming we survive out here and can send a message that we've got updates on the case.

"You know how to get to the Grundys' old house? If we're leaving these woods, I want to make a stop there."

"Sure." Harley stalked toward the pack he'd left leaning against a tree. "But right now, stay on my heels and keep your eyes peeled. I ain't slowin' down this time. Fast as we can go safely, we go."

Leo gestured to Mia and Emma to let him go first after the ranger, already adjusting his sights on the ground ahead. He fiddled with the Saint Jude pendant he always wore, rubbing the metal through his shirt even as he kept his eyes down.

Harley didn't have to tell him twice to get moving, and he was glad for the increased pace. But he wouldn't let anyone else fall in these woods. Not on his watch.

24
———

I pulled the boy forward, ignoring his little whine of fear. This wasn't the time.

The edge of the woods called, sun shining through the trees. I hadn't come this close to the border in a long time. There was no reason. But maybe my son needed to see where I'd come from.

Only bad memories are here. Nothing else. He'll see that. And he'll be better.

I gripped his arm tighter, pulling him behind me. The boy was crying like an infant. Sobbing and fussing as if he hadn't eaten or was freezing his tail off. He didn't know true cold, though. Not yet. And he needed to know what being my son truly meant. He didn't know that either.

At the edge of the trees, I stopped and looked out. As my dad would've said, "*I assessed the situation.*" Taking it in, I noted the street in front of the run-down home was empty. No cars and no people I could see. Still no nearby homes people might be spying from. Still no sign of anyone who didn't belong. It'd been a long time, and we'd taken hours to get here, but it seemed safe. For now.

"This better get through to you." I yanked on my son's arm, dragging him behind me as I hurried forward. The sun beat down on us, to punish us for coming here. Will sobbed, loud and stupid. I pulled him faster.

I didn't know why he couldn't get it through his head that I was just trying to help him.

At the porch, I kept my grip on him as I dug the key out from Mom's old flowerpot, now holding nothing but dead dirt and this rusty piece of metal. Maybe I should've taken it into the woods with me, but I didn't want to be staring at anything that tied me to this place.

The door still creaked open, same as always, and I pushed my son in ahead of me before slamming it behind us. The darkness was welcome after that short time in the sun. Dust exploded from under our feet as I pushed my son forward even more. Around us, the bones of an old life closed in, but I ignored them.

The thing to do was to keep moving.

"I'm going to show you what happened to the last bad boy."

He sobbed louder, gasping in air and stumbling.

"You cry like a baby. Stop!"

I kicked the door open and pushed him inside. He fell against my parents' bed. The boy's tears could've filled a river. It was disgusting, and I wondered if he could even be my son.

Strength was what I had. Strength and a will to survive.

This boy? He seemed to weaken with every passing minute.

My old son lay in the wooden box by the window. I walked around Will and yanked up the lid, leaned it against the wall, and stood back. Once my pride and joy, the bad boy now lay broken in his little coffin. His face was gone. I remembered when I came back and found animals eating him.

I had to take his head off then and never came back to put a new one on. The rock I used for his head was still there. Some of the skin from his face had been intact, so I'd stuck that on the rock. The moss I used for hair was all rotted, though.

Behind me, Will's crying shifted, going higher and then stopping. I looked down at him.

"Come here." I stomped my foot and pointed at the box holding my first attempt at having a son.

Will approached on his knees, crawling on the dirty floor.

"Stand up and walk."

Struggling to his feet, Will obeyed, and I felt good. I felt like he was learning. He would be a good son.

He came closer and looked inside.

A scream broke out, followed by a sob as Will fell backward on his useless ass. Tears dropped down his stupid cheeks all over again.

I dropped to my knees and grabbed his elbow before he could get any farther away. "Stop! I said to stop!"

My scream bounced off the walls around us, loud, and the boy shivered. I jerked his arm, staring down at him. How could he be so dumb if he was my son?

"You can avoid this! You can avoid being like the bad son! See him and be different!"

Will blinked at me, tears still falling. He was so stupid. So bad and stupid and wrong.

"Okay? Stop crying! All you have to do is pay attention and obey!"

"I...I..." He made a hiccup and coughed.

"Stop saying that! Stop breaking words! Speak like a real son!"

His lips shut, but the tears kept coming. He kept shaking

and tried to yank his arm from my grip, but I held tighter until he squealed. If he wanted to be my son, he had to learn. He had to learn *now*.

"I paid attention to my mom and dad. I obeyed them. And look how well I turned out! I survived. You can, too!"

The boy shivered, his eyes going soft like Mom's had when Dad would yell. I just had to hope I'd finally gotten through to him.

I shoved myself up from the floor and pulled him with me, spitting at my old son, who no longer served any purpose. I closed the lid on his useless body before dragging Will around the big bed to the door to my room.

Yanking the door open, I showed him the small space where I used to live. I had to sleep in the little room, under my parents' clothing hanging above me. That was all gone now, but my blankets were still in the corner, and so were my books.

"You want to live in here, like I did? Or do you want to be a good son?"

Around us, the old place seemed to laugh, as if the house knew Will could never be the son I needed him to be.

My whole body burned with shame and anger, being gawked at like that, made fun of by the old, evil place. It wasn't mocking Will or me. It was just a house that had made my parents do evil things, and the longer I stayed here with Will, the more I knew the house would make me do something evil too.

I couldn't let that happen. Not since I'd found my new son. Grabbing Will's arm, I pulled him out of the room. I slammed the door behind us and marched him down the little hall and out the door, slamming that shut behind me too.

Will's crying and moaning were making me angry, and I

almost dropped the key when I locked the door. I was so mad, and I knew I would never come back here again.

I threw the key into the grass and yanked Will along the porch.

We needed to get back to the woods, away from the stupid old house and my stupid old memories. We would go back to the woods, where things made sense. Where I could teach, and Will could learn. He'd learn to be my good son.

He had to.

When we got back to the cabin, he'd face the real test. My boy would connect, just like I had.

And when he passed that test, then he would really be my son.

25

Will knew he shouldn't scream like he was. Not again. He *knew* it. But he didn't want to go back to those woods. To the darkness and the endless trees and the smells and the blood. To being alone with this horrible person.

The man was getting angrier, gripping his arm like his hand was some kind of evil octopus tentacle, but Will dug his heels in and screamed for all he was worth. Ahead, the line of woods loomed, and his lungs burned as he fought, but he couldn't stop. The image of the man's last "son" was burned into his sight.

When the man tightened his grip, Will shrieked. He pulled at his sleeve, but the man kept walking, dragging him.

The old son was a doll he made out of skin. It was gross. Worse than some of the sideshow stuff at Mom's circus.

Will closed his eyes, still fighting the image of the skin doll back in that house. He could still smell it in his nose. It stank worse than the worst pile of garbage he'd ever smelled.

He had to help clean up the circus, when his dad was camping and his mom took him with her on the road. The trash could get so disgusting, all the old popcorn and half-eaten hot dogs. The skin doll was way worse.

The giant of a man yanked Will forward again. They were at the tree line, and he was being dragged back into the woods. He reached out, grabbing for anything he could hold onto, and caught hold of a sapling.

But the tree was so young and small, and the man was so big and strong, that the branches ripped off in his grip. He thought about hitting the man with them, but what good would that do? He'd probably just get angrier and tell Will he was being a bad son again.

He might take you back there and throw you in the box with the skin doll.

The man tugged him along. "Let's go, son. We have to go. Okay?"

"Why do you…" Will gasped, fighting down sobs as he dug his heels into the dirt. The forest was less than ten feet away now. "Why do you think I'm your son? Please, stop! Tell me!"

The man pulled him along, grunting with the continued effort. He smelled so bad. Will was used to it, but he *still smelled so bad*.

"What did you do with my real dad?" Will screamed at him and finally kicked the man's calf.

He swung around and stared at Will with his dark, vacant eyes.

"I'm sorry. I'm sorry," Will whimpered. "Please, don't put me in the box with the doll."

"That's good. You know what will happen if you're a bad son. Now walk." The man grunted and kept moving, his steps getting longer as they reached the trees.

Will allowed himself to be dragged. Thinking of his dad and all his lessons on surviving in the wild. What would he have said about this?

He couldn't recall a thing. All he could think about was the last time he'd seen his dad. This man and his dad had gone into their cabin, and there'd been shouting and the sounds of fighting. Will had been too afraid to go in, and as soon as he built up the courage, the huge man came out.

Alone.

And Will hadn't seen his dad since. That was days ago, maybe a week. He hadn't slept but a few hours here and there. Every time he asked to see his dad, the man got very angry.

Will's body went a little cold as they entered the shade of the woods, or maybe he was freezing from thinking about his father. It was hard not to for a bazillion reasons, the worst was…the man was wearing his dad's clothes. They fit well enough, though this man was taller.

What was his dad wearing? He'd asked that question and gotten a growl in return. He was scared to ask it again. To ask anything again.

Dad would've told me to stop asking. So I stopped asking most things, but why is this man calling me his son? I don't even know his name!

Will choked back another round of tears, stumbling as he was pulled along, and the toe of his sneaker caught on a raised tree root. He tripped but caught himself.

And then there was that hiker. Will was so happy to see him. He even thought maybe the hiker would help him get rid of this man and find his real dad.

But then, the madman killed him.

He'd never seen real murder before. On television and in movies and video games, when his mom got too busy to yell at him about how violence was bad, but not in real life.

I hope she doesn't come looking for me and Dad. This man will kill her, too, like the hiker.

Swallowing that thought, Will walked as fast as he could

to keep up with the man, if only to save his arm from being wrenched off. They were too far from that house for his screams to be heard now. And besides that, he hadn't seen anyone who might come rescue him.

His only hope was to calm down and find a way to escape. If he could calm down, maybe the man wouldn't hurt him…other than the bruise he'd undoubtedly left on his arm already.

Maybe the man wouldn't kill him like he'd killed those other people. If Will pretended he was his new son, he could convince the man to trust him. If he stayed calm and obeyed like he said, then, when he got his chance, he could run.

But the only problem with pretending to be the man's son was, well, a big one. Will didn't think he could kill anyone. Or take a bite out of their heart.

Not to mention this test the man was talking about. Will gagged at the thought of what it was, but as mad as the man had been that he wouldn't eat human meat…

Will could guess what the test would be.

26

Emma breathed easier once wider slivers of the midafternoon sunlight warmed her face and she glimpsed vehicles through the trees along the forest edge. But she refused to let her guard down. They'd navigated this stretch of wilderness better than she'd hoped, but the gruesome scenes they'd witnessed hung heavy over all of them.

The trek out of Buckskin had been thankfully uneventful. The rescue helicopter had come and gone, taking Ben and Laurie to safety. Emma hadn't been able to see their departure through the forest canopy, but the helicopter's rotors made their steady chop as it arrived and hovered, then soared away, taking the injured ranger and his partner back to civilization.

With Emma and the others on the lookout for traps and sabotaged trails, and the markers they'd left behind on their way in, Harley hadn't had much trouble leading them back out of the forest.

They'd even avoided the path where Ben had been injured and still got out in what felt like record time.

"Harley, we'd like you to lead us to the Grundy house

right away." Emma slid one pack strap off her shoulder, following him to his vehicle. "I know you'd like to be done, but—"

"I get it. I'll put this stuff away, but we gotta check in with the sheriff and see about Ben first."

Leo was already pulling out his phone as Harley began packing supplies. He put it on speaker. The sheriff answered on the first ring, and Leo's summation of events sounded even bleaker than they had in Emma's head for some reason.

The sheriff was less than pleased to hear the news.

"A whole room full of dismembered body parts? What in the hot, stinking hell is going on?"

"Wish we had the answer to that. For now, we're heading to the Grundy home. Evidence we found has us thinking there's a connection."

The sheriff remained silent for a few seconds, but when he spoke, his voice was rough with shock. "I'll have Laurie meet you folks there. Harley, you show them the way over and stay with 'em until she gets there. I believe she's still at the hospital."

Harley paused in what he was doing. "Fair enough. How's Ben?"

"Getting bandaged up," the sheriff grunted. "He'll be okay, I hear, but he's not great. Stubborn fool wants to be back at the office, but I told the doctor to keep him there."

Emma smiled for the first time since waking up from her unexpected visit to the Other. She hadn't thought Ben's wounds were fatal, but to hear that he was arguing with medical personnel was still something of a relief.

He's going to be okay. Maybe a little slower for a while, but alive.

The sheriff's voice grew muffled as he spoke to someone else, then he was back on their line. "Y'all be safe."

Within seconds, Harley had finished stowing away their

gear, and Emma led the way back to the SUV they'd driven over from their hotel. With Harley taking point in his vehicle and Leo driving theirs, the team moved out.

Both men drove more slowly than Emma would've liked, but they were soon bumping down a dirt road that ran along what she guessed was another perimeter of Buckskin Wilderness.

Scattered homes with old vehicles and rusting mailboxes dotted the road, though she wouldn't necessarily have called this a neighborhood. Gaps of several hundred feet stood between the houses. Many had hand-painted signs out front advertising the property for rent or sale.

Only one home had a newish car parked in front, but Emma spotted a heavy dent in one fender as they passed by. She was ready to suggest they stop to interview the residents when the familiar profile of a patrol car appeared up ahead.

Harley pulled in behind it, parking in front of a small home with peeling paint and a sagging front porch. A number of shingles hung from the eaves. Bare patches above them showed where the roof had succumbed to the elements.

Leo brought their vehicle to a stop behind Harley's and cut the engine. They exited and followed Harley to wait at the head of the drive.

Laurie trotted over from her patrol car and joined them.

"I knocked on every door I passed on the way in but haven't found anyone home yet. Nobody who wants to answer their door anyway." She waved at the house. "And this place has been empty since they were killed, so far as I know."

Emma eyed the shape of two ghosts shimmering into view near the door. Mr. and Mrs. Grundy, bloody and scowling. "Who owns the property?"

"The bank. It was up for sale for a while, some years ago, but nobody bought. Like most of the homes for sale out here, it sits and slowly gets reclaimed by the forest. There's a landscaping crew that comes by once a year to trim back trees and brush to create a fire break. They haven't been out yet, from the look of things." Laurie gazed out across the overgrown lawn. "Not exactly Grand Central in this town, and attracting people to buy a home where there were some gruesome deaths isn't easy anywhere."

Bracing herself for the cold, Emma led the way up the driveway after Harley said his goodbyes. Following Laurie, they made their way through dry, waist-high grass to reach the porch. She'd kept expecting the ghostly couple to approach, but they stood resolutely near their front window, which had long gone green with mold.

The woman had died by a gunshot to the head, and when Emma came within a few feet, she saw the man had lost the back of his own head to a bullet. They only glared at her, and if not for how they turned to watch her approach the house, Emma might've thought they hadn't even seen her.

Ate his gun after killing his wife. No wonder nobody wants to live here.

Emma felt their glares on her back, along with the cold of the Other, but fought off the sensation and focused on what they were there for.

At the front door, Laurie gloved up and let them in with a key she'd gotten from the bank. She shoved the door open while the agents put their gloves on.

Leo moved in first, announcing their presence. Emma was right behind him but couldn't hold back a cough. Mia came in after that.

They stood at the entrance of a small home with a living room to their right. The kitchen sat at the back, behind the narrow living room that held a faded, tattered sofa and small coffee table. A weathered dining table and chairs sat to the right of the sofa, against the far wall.

To their left, a short hall led to two doors. One hung open, revealing a bathroom. The other was closed.

Laurie scuffed her shoe through animal droppings beside the threshold. "Rats and squirrels, probably. Damn things find a way in, no matter how hard you try to keep 'em out."

Emma nodded, moving into the sitting area with the sofa as Leo stalked to the kitchen.

"No family photos." Emma eyed the stained, naked walls, not even seeing the outline of where a picture might have hung. She and Leo met up with Mia and Laurie near the short hallway. "Shall we?"

The air went colder at her back, and she glanced over her shoulder to see the Grundys standing by their dining table. Alan's ghostly white eyes glared at her. "Get out. This is none of your concern. None of y'all's."

"This is my house!" The ghostly woman beside him sneered as she stepped forward. "You people don't belong here!"

Emma blocked them out and held back a shiver.

They started with the bathroom, which had long since been taken over by mold. Mia backed away from the rotting, water-stained space. "We should have masks to protect ourselves from mold before we go in there."

"You bitch!" Denise Grundy screeched behind them, nearly deafening Emma. She flinched forward, and Leo raised an eyebrow at her. The ghost continued shrieking as Emma waved off Leo's concern, not wanting to give Laurie any reason to suspect she was seeing things that weren't there.

Even though you know for a fact that they are, Emma girl. Just get the search over with and get out of here.

The agents turned away from the mold-infested bathroom and faced the remaining door. It opened with a hard shove from Leo and Mia, revealing a king-size bed that had been stripped of any covers. Old bloodstains showed in the mattress, flooring, and wall. One corner of the mattress had been torn away, with tufts of stuffing and foam pulled out.

Possibly an animal got in and gnawed on the material.

Leo made his way inside for a quick search, heading toward the right where a bench sat beneath a window.

Across the room from the window, Mia opened the door to a closet.

Emma joined her, leaving Laurie in the hall. The ranger said she'd be outside, "In case any of the neighbors comes wandering by."

At the closet, Emma took in the decay and rot. Mold spread up from the floorboards to cover the walls. A mound of blankets sat in one corner, likely a nest for rats or whatever else might have found its way inside.

But the blankets had once belonged to a child. Even through the stains and filth, Emma could see the cartoonish images and shapes of a child's bedsheets.

Harley said they didn't have children. Maybe they lost one to miscarriage or...

But the more Emma looked at the rotting cloth, the less convinced she was that the Grundys had been childless. "Mia, can you shine a light on those blankets?"

Mia held out her phone's flashlight as Emma tentatively prodded the mound with her foot, revealing a sheaf of papers and some children's books. Everything was covered in mold and grime. Emma stooped to examine the items more closely and found another photograph, similar to the one they'd discovered earlier.

This one had no writing on the back, and the image showed the much younger Grundys standing outside their home. The husband held up a legal-size envelope, and a real estate agent's "SOLD" sign stood behind them in the center of the lawn.

Emma took a pen from her pocket and lifted the blankets aside to expose the papers more fully. She could just make out the text at the top of one page, identifying a real estate agent's office. The pages were all covered in flaking pieces of manila paper. A corroded envelope clasp sat at the bottom of the stack.

Leo's shout got her and Mia's attention. They spun to see him backing away from the window seat. He aimed a finger at it and covered his mouth with his other hand.

The chest by the window yawned at them, and Emma shifted closer. "What'd you find?"

Leo could only shake his head and march toward the door, exiting to the hall and taking deep breaths.

With Mia behind her, Emma went to the window seat, gagging as she saw the nightmare it held.

An oversize doll had been built and stitched together using human skin of varying colors. It had all been haphazardly connected with messy stitches of wire and yarn. The entire creation could have come from a horror-movie set.

But that is real skin, and those are real human hands, not props.

The torso was, thankfully, adult-sized, meaning whoever had made the bizarre object hadn't murdered a child in the process. Both hands were too large for the limbs they'd been stitched onto, but the arms themselves were just lengths of tree branches wrapped in human skin.

Same with the legs, one of which was missing a foot.

The head was just a large rock, with tatters of what may have been skin stuck to it. Bits and pieces of moss and leaf litter crowned the object, perhaps meant to represent hair.

Emma bent down by the trunk, even as Mia approached

with a curse. She probed the torso with her gloved fingers, wondering if she would feel ribs or more branches, like the ones that made up the limbs.

The desiccated skin broke beneath her fingertip, but instead of revealing viscera or bone, the hole she'd made showed stuffing. She looked to the shredded corner on the mattress, and her stomach turned over. "He skinned a man. Completely skinned someone and made a stuffed doll out of human flesh."

"He skinned multiple someones." Leo's voice was choked as he returned. "Look at the variation in color. That patchwork is from a lot of different skin tones."

Stepping away from the macabre sight, Mia spoke through a hand covering her mouth and nose. "Talk about nightmare fuel."

Emma could only nod, but more than the sight of this horror show was taking over her thoughts now. "The couple has been dead for far too long to have done this and…for us to find it in this condition. Someone else made this and is probably the one setting the traps and doing the killing."

"Heaven forbid it be two different people." Mia had come back to take pictures of the so-called skin doll with the rock for a head. "We're looking for the Grundys' adult child or someone close to them."

Emma gestured around the room. "I'd say they had a kid they kept secret. From what we found in that closet, that might have been the kid's 'room.' Either he's our killer, or knowing about him may lead us to the killer."

From the doorway, standing on either side of Leo, the Grundys screeched in unison. "Go away! Now!"

Laurie raced up behind Leo, gasping. "Someone heard a child screaming in the woods. We need to go!"

27

Outside the Grundy home, Laurie introduced them to a woman standing at the roadside, wringing her hands together. "This is Sasha Compton. She lives down the road, back toward Norell."

Emma moved forward and examined the woman. She wore a sweat-stained t-shirt and torn jeans.

"You reported hearing a child screaming?"

"Sure did. 'Least, I think it was a child. Could've been older kids playing around in the woods, but this one sounded frightened."

Emma zeroed in on the woman's hands as they clutched at each other in front of her abdomen. Her skin was scratched-up and smudged with dirt.

"Have you been working in your garden, Ms. Compton?"

"Huh?" She looked at her hands. "Yeah, I was pruning some rosebushes going wild at my place. The landscapers haven't come around yet, and I don't like all that vegetation blocking my walk."

"You don't wear gloves when you prune roses?"

She dug her hands into her pockets. "I came by because I saw your cars. Didn't think I'd be considered a suspect."

Emma smiled. "Why did our cars get your attention? Was there something you wanted to tell us about the child you heard?"

"I heard a boy screaming. Went looking for him, but I didn't find anyone." Sasha jerked her chin toward their cars. "I was just coming back out of the woods when I noticed y'all's vehicles and thought I'd say something."

Emma traded a glance with Leo, and he nodded, pulling out his notebook and writing down her name. "Have you seen children around here recently?"

"Ain't no kids living round here, but they come out this way on their bikes, from Norell. There's a creek not far into the tree line where there's good fishing."

"Did you see any bikes or fishing gear?"

Sasha eyed Leo, frowning. "Didn't see a thing. But I know what I heard, and people go missing in those woods. I've seen the news."

And we've seen more than that, at this point.

"Could you make out any words?" Mia prompted her. "Anything specific that you remember when you heard the screaming?"

The woman leaned back on her heels and lifted her chin. "I'm not sure, mind you, but I thought I heard a boy crying, 'Let me go.' That's why I took off like I did, faster'n I've moved in ages. But I'm just not sure. Mostly, I just heard screaming."

Emma's heart had begun pounding faster, spurring her to go search, but without a voice to follow and no clear direction, this wasn't a lot to go on.

Harley pulled his vehicle into the driveway just then, and he climbed out a moment later with a scowl and a wave. "Laurie texted me to come back. Someone heard screaming?"

Emma nodded, glad to see the tracker had been close enough to reach them before they'd set out.

"You folks need anything else from me?" Sasha glanced back and forth between them, then over Emma's shoulder at the abandoned house with the gaping front door.

"We're good, Sasha, thanks." Laurie patted her on the shoulder, but Emma and the others were already heading into the backyard.

No clear path led from the property into the woods. Buckskin formed a boundary along the entire length of the small community, and although Emma could count a dozen spots where they might easily slip into the woods, she saw no sign of recent passage.

Then again, she wasn't a trained tracker. "Harley, does anything back here show signs of recent human passage?"

He'd been examining the tree line at the back of the Grundy property, directly behind the house. Stooping, he lifted a broken sapling branch. "This was pulled off within the last hour, I'd say. Cambium layer is still showing green, and it's got a broken spiderweb hanging off. I'm seeing disturbed leaf litter and soil all through this area, so this is where we go."

On the other side of the tree line, gloom huddled beneath the branches, no longer chased away by overhead sunlight. Emma shivered. She did not want to go back in there.

But the life of a little boy depended on them.

Harley stalked forward, yelling over his shoulder. "Let's get this over with, but keep your eyes out for traps and snakes. If you see any downed branches bigger than your arm, a copperhead could be sleeping on the other side. I'll take the lead up the middle here."

Emma thought to argue as he disappeared into the woods but didn't. They were lucky the man was helping. He'd been so antsy to get out of there earlier. Looking at the others, she determined their search plan. "Let's spread out. I'll head to the right with Leo. Mia and Laurie, go left? We all search for twenty minutes and meet back here. Yell if you find anything."

Without giving herself time to doubt the search order she'd given, Emma moved into the woods with Leo just behind her. She could only content herself with thinking that this stretch of the terrain was flat, and they wouldn't go far in fifteen or twenty minutes. Their cell phones would work if they needed backup.

Walking beside her, Leo glued his gaze to the ground for traps, and they kept quiet by mutual agreement. They needed to hear Will if he yelled out again.

She shifted a branch higher to move underneath, and the air went cold around her. Thick with the Other. For a moment, she feared the woman from her vision was overtaking her again and that she'd pass out, but Denise Grundy appeared at her elbow. Despite the woman's glare, Emma relaxed and kept searching.

"You all need to get gone! I know you hear me!" The ghost paced Emma, walking through trees and bleeding from her forehead. "Go away!"

Now Alan Grundy appeared directly in front of Emma as she stepped over a dry creek bed, one eye on the leaves and searching for traps. "My wife knows what she's talking about, lady. Even if she was dumber than a brick in life."

"Clam up, you bastard. You shot me because you couldn't bring yourself to admit you didn't know how to raise a boy."

Alan Grundy turned on his wife. "And you did? It was your idea to hide him from the world, to keep him a secret."

Ignoring their bickering, Emma continued walking. She never got straight answers from ghosts when she tried anyway.

Alan spun on her and matched her pace, walking

backward. He leveled a finger at her. "You don't know what you're doing. There's strength in isolation." He puffed himself up, hands on hips, and raised his voice.

His wife chimed in now, seeming to agree with him instead of opposing his every word. "Isolation builds character! Maybe you should be alone too."

Pausing momentarily, Emma stared at them. "Are you worried about your son?"

Leo froze beside her, mid-step, but his eyes narrowed. He kept quiet, watching her.

"It's the Grundys," she spoke quietly, watching the ghosts and still trying to keep an ear out for any far-off screams, "and they want us to go away."

The woman glared, cheeks reddening, and the man began repeating what he'd already told her. Nearly screaming at her now, so that Emma flinched backward before she could stop herself.

When he paused for a breath, she met his blank gaze and spoke flatly. "I'm not leaving these woods. You want me alone, you go away."

Leo's lips quirked as if he were hiding a smile, and Emma took some courage from it. They were in this together, especially now that he knew her secret.

Emma held her gaze on the dead couple, daring them to continue arguing. Finally, the Grundys shivered out of view, and Emma released a deep breath as the cold of the Other faded around her.

Leo seemed to read what the release of tension in her body meant, and he glanced around. "They're gone. Right? I'm guessing, but you visibly relaxed just now."

She nodded. "Yeah, they're gone."

"They give you anything we can use?"

"Just a lot of yelling about wanting us gone and us not

knowing what we're doing. Talked about strength in isolation, though, and building character."

Leo's look soured. "Sounds like something an abusive parent might say."

"Just what I was thinking. And the way the woman looked when I mentioned a son, I think we're on the right track with our killer being their kid, even if they didn't admit it." Emma grabbed a stick and poked at a pile of dead leaves in front of her. The couple's attitude still bothered her, though.

The ghosts hadn't seemed protective of their son at all. Their property, maybe, but more than anything, they'd just seemed spiteful. Like they wanted to bother her.

Or maybe they were protecting their son by distracting me. I couldn't have heard Will over their yelling.

Mia's voice echoed out over the woods. "I heard him! I heard him!"

Emma fought the urge to sprint toward her friend. Instead, she grabbed another stick and began taking a two-handed approach to clearing the way ahead of her, searching for traps as she went while Leo kept his attention on the branches above, looking for any collapsing traps like the first one they'd found.

Somewhere ahead, she heard someone crashing through the woods. If that was Mia and she wasn't keeping an eye out for traps…

"Be careful! Remember to watch your steps!"

She heard Harley echo the warning from somewhere ahead, but whoever was running didn't stop, and Emma tried to speed her own steps while still being careful.

Mia was just visible through the trees when the scream rang out. High-pitched and agonizing, it echoed over the three of them just as Harley moved into view, pale and stricken.

"That had to be Laurie." His whisper died as they turned toward the scream, moving as a group.

Mia pushed back a tree branch. "She ran off when we heard him." Her voice shook. "I couldn't stop her!"

Ahead, they could hear Laurie sobbing and gasping from somewhere within the forest. "Help! Please!" Her voice trailed off into whimpers that echoed.

When they found her, blood pooled around her over a stretch of leaves and soil and greenery. She lay face down, arms akimbo like she'd fallen forward while walking and been unable to brace her fall.

Wordlessly, Leo pointed toward her feet, where a trip wire could be seen stretched between two trees.

Emma knelt beside her, listening to the woman gasp for air. On her other side, Harley crouched to the forest floor to try to see where the blood was coming from, and then he let out a low curse.

"Bastard tripped her onto a knife that was set up to catch someone. Blade's—"

"My chest," Laurie whimpered, "my chest. Can't breathe."

Leo had his phone out. "Calling medevac. Can we do anything for her until they get here?"

He was talking to someone a second later, telling them the situation. Emma shoved herself to her feet and stepped backward, turning away from Laurie's prone form. She had seen the truth in Harley's face. He didn't expect her to survive this injury.

Mia had moved around behind Harley, and she raised her stricken expression to Emma, shaking her head.

Harley had bent down beside Laurie and was whispering into her ear, trying to calm her and do what he could to keep her steady until help arrived.

Leo moved back into the woods at a slow walk, the phone

still to his ear as he promised to lead the paramedics straight to them.

28

Emma stared past Leo and Mia to where Harley was talking to the medevac pilot. A team of two were loading Laurie into the helicopter whipping at the tall grass beyond the tree line. The Grundys' property was so overgrown, the pilot had to hover and lower a stretcher.

The ranger was still hanging on, but Emma didn't have much hope, considering the horrific chest wound she'd suffered.

Mia paced behind Leo, eyes locked on the woods as she argued. "We have to keep searching. He can't have gotten too far away."

Emma sighed. "With all the time between hearing Will's voice and now, there's no telling which direction he would've been taken in."

Mia grimaced. "We could keep looking for those *X*s, but—"

Harley came up behind them. "No point. Ben's injury put a fire under the ass of the ranger service. They sent drones and choppers over each set of coordinates and didn't find a single cabin."

The cold of the Other encased Emma again, and the blond ghost from before appeared behind Harley, guts pouring from his bloody abdomen, his expression sagging. He shook his head. "Too far gone. Too far gone."

She fought the urge to tell him to say something helpful or go away, but Leo's phone rang. He answered and put it on speaker.

"Leo, this is Ben Carter." Leo's eyebrows rose, and he held the phone between them before answering.

"How are you—"

"I'm fine. And we don't have time for that." A nurse could be heard saying something in the background, but the ranger shushed her. "I got a call from a guy who says his husband, Burt Wilcox, came out to hike a couple of days ago. The caller, Charles Renner, was away on business and just got home. He expected Burt to be there, and he's worried sick about him. Looks like we have another missing person."

The ghost beside Leo let out a breathy sob, and to Emma's surprise, he started to shake visibly. "I'm so sorry, Charlie. I'm so, so sorry. You were right."

They'd found the missing hiker, it seemed. Long before they'd even known to look for him.

Wetness stung Emma's eyes, and she stared at the helicopter, now rising away with Laurie inside.

Leo continued talking to Ben, learning that the dead hiker and his husband had been together for years. Beside her and Leo, the ghost now known as Burt shook with sorrow that Emma fought not to reflect.

Leo hung up after that.

"Maybe we could follow him," Emma spoke as soon as the call had ended, "if he...just left."

She gazed at Burt, but he was too focused on his grief to be of any help at the moment.

Harley frowned. "This latest lost hiker, you mean?"

"Right. If he just left a couple of days ago, there are probably still signs of where he went. Footprints, broken sticks, like you found here. Could you help us track him? Maybe we can figure out where the killer took him." She spoke carefully, knowing she couldn't outright tell Harley the ghost was beside them. "We have to assume the killer found him, if he's been gone this long and Charlie's that distraught."

Leo cocked his head at Emma. "Charlie?"

"We already have the killer's recent trail!" Mia gestured frantically at the woods behind the property. "He was right here with Will Payne!"

But Harley was already shaking his head. "If we assume this house was his, he's probably been in and out of this area a dozen times. And if there was any spot he'd expect to be tracked from, it'd be this one. Chances are, there's a dozen different false pathways and untold booby traps in the woods immediately surrounding this property. It's a miracle Laurie was the only one who got injured just now."

Leo held his phone up. "The ground around here is flatter than a lot of Buckskin's terrain. We can get helicopters and drones diverted to search this area. Maybe call in some rangers from local areas to help."

Cowed, Mia caught her breath and stepped back, which gave Emma a chance to plug her plan again. She had Burt on her side, after all. "This is the best chance we've got, guys. We go to Burt Wilcox's car, and we move into the forest from there—"

"We already know where his lair is." Harley ran one hand through his long hair, betraying the frustration all of them felt. "We can head there with backup and—"

"Those were old bodies, Harley," Emma countered.

"She's right, man," Leo confirmed, eyeing her intently.

Emma stepped away from Burt, trying to speak gently to the group as a whole. "Nobody there had been dead for less than a week. Somewhere out there, Steven Payne built himself a new shack, and I'm willing to bet that's where our killer is operating from, whoever he is."

Burt was shaking less visibly, and he even looked… hopeful, something, maybe just a little relieved.

Emma gave him a small nod. "Remember all those plans? Even if Payne didn't ultimately build in one of those marked locations, he was absolutely building a cabin somewhere. We just have to find it."

Mia shook her head and turned away.

Leo nodded. "I buy that."

Emma sighed. Much as she felt this was the right choice, the idea of heading back into those woods was as much of a nightmare as the doll inside the home at their backs. "Let's call Ben back and see if Charlie knows which trailhead Burt started from."

And then it's back into those woods. With our eyes wide open… or else.

29

Emma met Harley's eyes even as Leo called Ben back. "What about it? Do you think you can track him?"

"Well, it did storm three days ago, and it hasn't rained since. The soil will still be soft enough that we'll find spoor."

Behind him, Burt Wilcox's ghost wavered in the air, bloody chest open wide, intestines swaying. Emma pulled her gaze away from the crying ghost and stared at Harley. "Sounds like you meant to say something else, but you're holding back. What do you need to tell us, Harley?"

He shook his head. "I signed up to be a ranger, not an FBI agent. What happened to Ben and Laurie…I don't want to end up like that."

"We got out safe before, and we left markers on our trails in and out." Leo moved in to stand with them, his voice sounding stronger than Emma felt about the idea. She was thankful for the support. "There's a ten-year-old boy's life at stake here."

"Yeah, I know there is." He sighed, and then reached both hands back and tightened his ponytail in the same way another man might have rolled up his sleeves to get to work.

"And you're right that it changes things. But there are no guarantees as to when we can move. Depending on which trailhead the man started out from, that's what'll determine the supplies we need and whether there's any point in heading out tonight and making camp or just holding off until morning."

Leo's phone buzzed. "This is Agent Ambrose."

A second later, he'd put it on speaker and held it up so all of them could hear. "I'm Ranger P.K. Mitchard. I have Charles Renner with me. You'd like to speak to him?"

A panicked voice broke through louder than the ranger's. "Are you cops?"

"We're FBI." Leo paused there, as if waiting for some reaction, but they were only met with silence.

Emma met Mia's gaze and could see they had the same question. Was the man more worried or reassured by Leo's response?

She leaned forward toward the phone. "Tell us about Burt, Charlie."

"He went into the wilderness Tuesday morning, the day after I went away for a work conference. He was supposed to be back Tuesday night and should have been here when I got home this afternoon. I always worry about him, and I had a bad feeling about him leaving this time. He knows what he's doing, but—"

"Ranger Mitchard again here. I hate to say it, but Mr. Wilcox's car is at the trailhead Mr. Renner identified as his husband's usual starting point. He must be still up in the woods."

Harley spoke up, introduced himself, and then went on. "Mitchard, can you tell us exactly where you are? And, Mr. Renner, do you know what supplies Burt took into the woods? Was he prepared to be gone a few days?"

The ranger recited a road and mile marker that meant

nothing to Emma, but Harley nodded as if he knew just the place and jotted something down on his phone. Their resident ghost plopped himself down on the ground and stared at his hands. Emma tried to ignore the way his intestines bled out of his stomach as he hugged himself.

Charlie's panicked voice came back on the line. "Burt always prepared for at least two days, even when he'd go for just a few hours. You gotta understand, he *always* makes it home when he says he will. He knows I worry, and especially when I'm out of town. Burt wouldn't do this to me. He wouldn't."

On the ground at Emma's feet, Burt's ghost shook his head, tears pouring down from his white eyes. "I wouldn't, Charlie. I wouldn't. I'm so sorry. So, so sorry."

Emma tried to focus on the phone, regretting all the times she'd wished a ghost would stick around a bit more than they had, because Burt was ripping her heart out.

"He was gonna do a one-day hike. Maybe ten, twelve miles total, he said." Charlie's breath shuddered. "We live about an hour away from where he parked. He should've been home Tuesday night."

"Did you try to reach him, to confirm he'd come home?"

Sobbing came across the line before Charlie spoke again. "The conference was a retreat up in the mountains. We didn't have cell service until this morning, when we left for the airport. I called before I boarded and left him a message. Burt hates using phones. He'd always get back to me, though."

Turning away from the phone, Emma focused on Harley. The man confirmed Burt Wilcox's description with Charlie.

Leo lifted an eyebrow in Emma's direction, and she nodded. Charlie's description of his husband matched the ghost perfectly.

They'd identified the victim. And they still needed to find his killer.

30

I looked at my son, still acting scared but not crying now. "You ready for a test?"

My question was stupid, but I asked anyway. The boy stared at our firepit, where the piece of rebar I used as the roasting spit lay nearby. I'd removed the base of the old spit because it was well past time.

And Will had to know what it took to survive out here. "When you eat someone, they become a part of you. You connect, and you want what's best for them, just like they would if things were the other way."

Will swayed in the dirt, staring up at me. "I don't understand."

Grinding my teeth, I backed off and went into the cabin. Our last catch had been a good find, and I'd saved his torso, arms, and upper legs for just this moment. The lower legs had been a decent meal, but this would be better.

I pulled the body from where it had been hanging over the counter, wrapped in the safety blanket he'd had with him.

Just like my dad had always said. *"Gotta protect our*

provisions, son. That's how we live and thrive." My boy would learn that, too, sooner than later.

Outside, I placed the remains—still in their blanket—on a large rock near Will. I'd taken pains to move it there just for this purpose. He shifted as if the meat might bite him, and I kicked at his leg to regain his attention.

"Son. Look at me."

Gaping like a fish, he did.

"You have to respect their remains by mounting them, cooking them like they deserve. And ya do it here in the forest, so they're a part of it forever. Connected to you and the land."

He trembled, holding his knees. "I don't want to be part of them forever. Or here forever."

I crouched in front of him, and I spoke as my dad would have, as my son deserved. "Are you a good son? Or a bad son?"

His eyes went flat. But then he nodded. "A good one."

The grin that came to my lips was bigger than any I'd offered, and it scared him—because he wasn't used to it, clearly—but that was just what I'd been waiting for.

My son knew. He knew what was needed.

"If you're going to live like your dad, you have to know how to build a spit and put a body on it. Right?"

Will blinked repeatedly, but then he nodded, and I waved for him to stand up. The boy was slow to take direction, but he could learn. I knew he could.

Taking his arm, I pulled him over to the side of the cabin, where a tall stack of wood sat waiting. The axe nearby was half as tall as the boy, but he had to learn. I handed it to him, haft first, and pointed at the wood. "Cut up thick those pieces of wood into narrow ones. Then you have to nail them together to make the base for a spit. Three pieces together, each side, and the rod rests on top. The spit has to be big enough to keep a large piece of meat off the ground."

Moving like a machine, Will pulled pieces of wood down off the pile. One by one, he chopped them, and I could tell he'd learned this part well already. Watching his first dad, no doubt. That was good.

He chopped, chopped, and chopped some more, until I began to wonder if he was putting off the rest of the chore.

When he stopped to breathe, I reached out and gripped the axe before he could argue. "That's enough. Okay. Next step. You take that hammer and the nails over by the fire, and you build a spit base."

He stared back toward the pit as if frozen, hands clenched. I was about to grab him and yank him over to the tools when he looked up at me. "Can I see the old one? So I can remember how it looks?"

That seemed fair. Learning by example was how my dad had taught me.

I led him to the other side of the cabin and pulled him beyond the flytrap head. We went into the bushes where I'd left the old spit to rot. The boy stared at it.

Reminds me of me when I'm figuring out a new trap. That's good.

"Good boy." I grinned at him, and even if he didn't look at me, I saw him jerk back and take the good words in. He knew. "Okay, son. Now let's get this done."

Will moved back around the cabin, not looking at the head I'd left outside, but that was okay. We'd get him there later. Tomorrow maybe, or whenever we caught one of those people snooping around, trying to take my boy from me.

The hammer hung loose in his hand. Limp. I stomped my boot into the dirt nearby, and he flinched back and looked up. "Hold your arm straight, son! Straight!" I called up thoughts of my dad, thinking of his old lessons. "Grip it tight and hold it straight and hit fast. Okay?"

He gulped, but then he looked back down at what he was doing. Soon, he began to build.

I went around the firepit and sat down by the body. This would be good, strong food for us, just like my new son was good and strong. "Once you have the spit together, we have to tie wire around the man's body to hold his arms in. Holding him to the rod is the hard part, but you can do it."

The boy didn't look at me. Just kept focused. That was okay. Not a bad thing.

"I'll help you raise the spit, but that's all I'll help you with. You have to learn to do all this yourself, but it takes a lot of muscle to raise the spit." I held out my arm, flexing for the boy, but he only blinked at me before going back to his work. "Once the spit's up, you have to start the fire."

The boy nodded again. His hands shook, and it took him three tries to hit each nail once, but he was getting there.

If my son could do this, we could have a good life together in these woods. There'd be more than enough for the two of us to live well.

The next lesson after this would be traps. I would show him, as many times as I had to, just how to build them and snare our prey. And he would learn.

Soon, the boy would be able to live by himself out here if he had to.

If he can do it. If he can pass this test and learn to make traps.

I shifted, smelling the sweat of the boy. He was nervous. Scared like an animal. But I knew he could pass these tests.

He had to.

If he failed, that would mean he was a bad boy, just like my old son. And if he was like my old son, I'd have to punish him. Worse than my other son, but he'd end up in the same place if things came to that.

And I knew I had the strength to punish him. But I hoped Will didn't make me do that.

I wanted Will to be a good son. To pass these tests…and connect.

31

Will channeled his mom, thinking of how she stayed calm even when she had clients who, as she said, gave her the creeps "with their dark energy." She'd be calm now, no matter how scared she was.

I used to be scared when she was telling fortunes. But then I learned. I got better. She'd want me to do what he says and come back to her. I have to.

And that meant he had to stay calm. No matter how much the man talked and muttered about his old son and his new son.

His hands shook at the thought of what he was working up to.

"Be more careful!" the man barked at him, digging his heels into the dirt, and Will bit back his own cry. "Okay? Okay!"

The crazy man said *okay* more than anyone Will had ever met. If Will got out of this, he vowed never to use the word again. Nothing was *okay* about eating other people.

Will hit his thumb with the hammer. He dropped the nail and pulled back. Tears threaded through his eyelashes as he sucked on the digit, but one glance at the man made him yank his finger from his mouth. His eyes were dark. Hateful. "I'm sorry. I'm sorry."

"Don't do that. That's for babies! Okay?"

Nodding, Will said, "Okay," which made the man relax. He picked up the hammer and went back to work. He took a deep breath, steadied a new nail, and hit it dead center, just like he'd been taught.

Will's dad—his *real dad*—had always told him that when there was an emergency, you sometimes had to do hard stuff. Painful stuff. Will was going to give this everything he had, despite how horrifying his situation was. This was an emergency, after all.

If he didn't do what the man wanted him to, he knew he wouldn't survive.

Plus, he knew how to do a lot of this stuff. The man had taken some supplies from the hikers, but a lot of them had come from his dad's own cabin. The hammer was familiar in his hands, and these were the same nails he'd used to help his dad with the table inside.

He'd sawed lots of wood for the cabin and helped with furniture too.

Now the spit was done, so he sat back on his heels, staring at it. The next part was what he'd been dreading.

The man kicked a roll of wire toward him, along with wire cutters. He pointed at the emergency blanket and the body it covered, a reminder of what Will had to do now.

The easy part came first. He moved the two bases he'd built to the edges of the firepit, where they'd wait for the rebar…and what they were meant to support.

Will looked up at the killer who called him his son. "Do you have gloves?"

The man frowned. "You mean so I won't cut myself on the wire?"

Please, please, please. I don't want to touch the blood.

The man shook his head, and sour bile rose up in Will's throat. Then he thought of his dad's old supplies. "There's gloves in the cabin. By the door. I could use those? I just... really don't want to cut myself."

For a second, Will thought the man would disagree, and he began bracing himself for the feel of the dead man's slick, hairy, cold skin. But the killer shoved himself to his feet and stalked over to the cabin. By the time he came back with gloves, Will had calmed his beating heart and began, once again, to remind himself to channel his mother.

He could do this. He *must* do this.

The gloves were big on him, his father's size, but they made him feel a little better.

Act like Dad's with you. It's kind of like he is, wearing these. Pretend he's helping you. He always said he was with you even when he wasn't. Remember that. You can do this.

Eyeing the girth of the body and arms, still wrapped in the bloody blanket, Will measured out a length of wire. Then he moved the rod over and propped it beside the rock where the body lay. Carefully, he caught one corner of the blanket between his thumb and finger and peeled it up and away from the corpse.

With a silent apology and a prayer for forgiveness, Will kept tugging.

As the last of the blanket came away, he closed his eyes and took three deep breaths. Will wished the dead man could come back to life and help him fight the crazy cannibal man. That would be the ultimate joke, he thought, to have the dead man turn into a zombie and take a bite out of the person who killed him.

"Hey!" The crazy man snapped his fingers to get Will's attention. "Wake up. Not done, okay?"

Will turned. The killer was staring at him, squint-eyed, as he mouthed, *Okay, okay,* and nodded for Will to keep going.

"Okay, okay." *Fucking okay!*

Saying the f-bomb in his head almost made him giggle, but he didn't think the man would like that, so he stayed quiet.

"I know knots." First, he laid the rebar down the length of the man's body. Will measured out another length of wire, and worked to wrap it around the body, pulling it underneath and working it back and forth to get it around the shoulders. "I don't wanna take any chances, okay, so I think a square knot should be what I do, not a simple overhand knot."

The man leaned closer, and Will kept babbling. He didn't mention his dad, or how his dad had taught him four different knots, or how proud he and his dad had been when he'd mastered them. He just babbled on and on about what the different knots were used for, thinking back to his dad as he wrapped the body and prepared it for the fire.

He didn't let himself look at the man, not the dead one or the very-much-alive one who was watching him. Will focused on the wire and the square knots, forcing his hands to move carefully with the wire, the body, and the cutters.

He thought of his dad, tried to hear his voice to guide him.

"Now, Will, this is a square knot. It's real good for binding things." His dad leaned in beside him, keeping the ropes within the circle of firelight.

Will tried to pay attention, but he wanted another s'more, and another hot dog, too, now that he thought about it.

"Like what?" He sat straighter.

"Oh, like 'most anything. It's also called a reef knot, and sailors use it a lot on ships. This was a big one for the pioneers, too, and when you and I go camping, you're gonna need it all the time. We'll

use it to tie our cooler into the trees and keep bears from getting our food. You don't want a bear to eat all our food, do you?"

This was just "practice camping," with their home a dozen yards away and music playing on the porch.

His dad held up the ropes, making sure he saw every move in the fire's glow. "See this? You hold one end of the rope in each hand. You start with the right one...that's your working end. You cross that over the left end, like this, and loop 'em around. Now you have an overhand knot. Then you do the same thing but use the left hand as your working end. Got it? Here's a trick to help. Right over left, left over right, makes a square knot good and tight."

Will nodded, though he wasn't sure he had it. As he worked his own rope, he recited the rhyme his dad used. "Right over left, left over right, makes a square knot good and tight." And if he got it right...more s'mores!

"That's all that matters." His dad met his eyes. "We practice everything together, right? Pals forever. I'll help you 'til you get it right."

Will pulled the ends tight around the dead man's legs, tying them to the spit now too. His dad's old rhyme repeated in his head like a mantra, steadying his hands. "Right over left, left over right, makes a square knot good and tight."

"What's that, son?"

Shit.

He hadn't realized he'd said that out loud. Will swallowed and shoved the memory down deep. He'd been awfully hungry in the past—his mom said growing boys were—but right now, Will didn't think he'd ever be hungry again.

The rod with its horrifying cargo lay on the big rock near the firepit.

Nearby, the killer grinned at him, visibly pleased. Standing back to look at it, Will tried to judge the shape and the weight. He examined his knots closely, then cut more wire and used two more long loops to anchor the midsection.

Bad as this was, it would be a lot worse to have to do it all over again.

He bit back bile, wiping his gloves against each other and praying the man didn't think to tell him to take them off now that the wire-cutting was all done. Will still didn't want to touch the body, and as hard as it might've been to tie knots while wearing gloves, compared to touching a mutilated dead body, the extra effort had been worth it.

"I think we're ready to raise it."

"Okay!" The man bounced to his feet so fast that Will flinched backward, but he only moved over to the side of the spit holding the man's shoulders. "I'll take this end. It's heavier."

Will took the offer for the kindness it was and braced himself before gripping onto the spit below the man's limp thighs.

"Okay, one, two, three!" The man lifted so fast that he nearly carried the whole load, and Will along with it, to the fire.

Will fought to keep up and keep his grip, and he just managed. He steadied the spit as the man piled rocks around one leg and then tossed more rocks on the second leg too. It didn't look as steady as Will would've liked, but the man seemed pleased.

"Okay. Now you build the fire."

Will knew how to build a fire. That was something else his dad taught him.

He laid the gloves carefully aside, wondering what excuse he'd use if the man demanded he touch the body again. For now, though, it was better to work without them, especially since he didn't want the work gloves to catch on fire.

Carefully, slowly, he gathered little branches for kindling.

The man had only used flint and steel to build a fire in front of Will, and although there was a lighter inside, Will figured the basic tools were what he'd have to use too. But that was fine. All those nights spent camping out here and building their forever cabin were helping Will through this.

With tinder and kindling in a loose pile, just how his dad would've done it, Will bent to his task. He tried to breathe in the dirt and the woods instead of the blood and rotting flesh. He focused on the tools in his hands, the roughness of the flint and the hot, smooth steel.

Will went to work fast, scraping the flint above the tinder against the steel rod. The sparks came fast, just like they should, and relief flooded him.

He bent closer to the fire and blew little puffs of air, nursing the fire the way his dad had taught him.

Above him, the man stomped his feet in celebration, shaking dirt into Will's precious fire, but he kept working.

"Okay, good, son! Good!"

The man gripped Will tight and pulled him up into a bloody-smelling bear hug that left him breathless.

Somehow, he managed not to scream.

32

Emma chewed on another piece of dried peach, still cradling the unopened bag of nuts that Leo had passed her way from his spot near the campfire. She should've been hungry after three full hours of hiking and searching, but her movements were little more than mechanical.

She needed to eat, so she would…but her stomach would've preferred otherwise.

The darkness around them harbored not just ghosts and a missing child now, but also an actual cannibal. And although it was only around nine at night, the creepiness factor made it feel like midnight on Halloween. She chewed, focusing on the dried fruit in her rations, and prayed that Laurie's ghost wouldn't show up next.

Ever since darkness had fallen, Emma's subconscious had begun expecting her, though as deep in the woods as they'd come, they'd yet to hear any more news about her condition. But if she did die, Emma was sure she'd be the first to know.

Drones had buzzed around the area until sunset, but now the only sounds were the crackling of their campfire, insects, and the haunting silence that surrounded them.

No wonder humanity started building cities. There's nothing between us and whatever wild animals, or wild people, are out here looking for food.

Across from Emma, Mia took mouse-sized bites from an MRE. Between them, Leo stared upward into the brilliant night sky as if it might hold the answers to the universe. Only Harley displayed any life as he tore into a piece of jerky. He caught Emma's eye, offering her a bag of the stuff, and her stomach flipped.

"I'm good, Harley, thanks." She pulled her gaze from the dried meat in his hands, struggling to separate the image from those dried body parts she'd seen in the shack earlier. But the teeth marks in that leg overlaid her every thought.

What do you have to go through to turn to eating humans?

The question clogged her brain as she sucked overly sweet flavor from a piece of dried pineapple. She wasn't sure she wanted an answer to that question.

Leo popped a small handful of nuts into his mouth, nodding at the ones in Emma's hand. When he'd swallowed, he cleared his throat to get her attention. "I know none of us have much of an appetite, but you need more than fruit."

Harley grunted as he tore off another piece of jerky and chewed. It rested in the side of his cheek as he continued where Leo left off. "We'll need our strength if we're gonna find that boy tomorrow. And if we're endangering our lives on his behalf, I damn well plan to find him. He's out here somewhere."

And we want to not just find him but also avoid getting killed in the process.

Branches cracked in the distance, and Emma couldn't help jerking to the side in reaction, staring off into the dark. Being paranoid was better than observing their guide tear into dried meat anyway.

When Emma turned back to the fire, Mia nodded at her.

"Every time I hear something, I think it must be our killer. I know there's wildlife out here, but…"

"Dark's getting to you all." Harley swallowed down some water and gazed around their group. "Remember, this fire won't scare any animals off. They might come sniffing around for warmth. You're gonna hear them. We'll keep a watch out tonight, but don't let the paranoia keep you from resting."

Leo leaned forward and added some more kindling to the fire, though his eyes were on the two tents off to the side. One he'd share with Harley, and the other was for her and Mia. "After nine hours of walking? My eyes'll be closed before I hit the sleeping bag."

Harley nodded and then shoved himself up from the rock he'd perched on. "We'll call it a night soon. I'm gonna go take a look around and use the facilities. Stay together."

"Eyes open," Emma gave the reminder automatically, "and we'll be here."

Harley had waited at the edge of the fire for them to acknowledge the warning, but now he trekked off into the dark. His light disappeared slowly, illustrating the care he took with each step even now, after they'd scouted their campsite for at least twenty feet in every direction.

Mia sighed, picking at some nuts in her hand. "The smell of his jerky nearly made me gag."

"Same." Emma eyed her friend, then lowered her voice and leaned closer to her and the fire. "How are you doing anyway? This is a hell of a case to come back to."

"Ha." Mia ate a few nuts, considering the question. Her eyes sparkled in the firelight, but Emma could still see the exhaustion. They all felt it at this point. "I'm struggling, I guess. But it's not being back. It's today…I'm not even a hundred percent sure I heard Will, now that I really think about it. What if I didn't? And it was me yelling out that got Laurie hurt. Maybe killed. It feels like Vance all over again."

Emotion stopped up in Emma's throat, and she could only shake her head. It hadn't even occurred to her that Mia might be thinking like that.

Leo reached out and gripped her arm, holding on until she finally looked at him. "You didn't lure Vance into that building. Your kidnappers did."

"And today," Emma spoke over the fire, willing her voice to remain steady, "you didn't do anything wrong. I know you. If you thought you heard Will, you did. We all yelled for Laurie to stop running, to be more cautious. That's all you could've done."

Mia shrugged, eyes down. "I'm sure I could've been more."

"We're trying to save a child." Emma reluctantly stuck another piece of dried fruit into her mouth. "It's not like you were the one who put traps out in those woods either. And you didn't tell her to run. Whatever happens to Laurie, it's on the killer. Not you."

Leo shifted on the log he'd been occupying and spoke softly. "Guilt's a hell of a thing, Mia. We all get it. If you need anything, you know we're here."

"I know." Mia wiped her hands together, dropping a few last nuts to the ground. "And I appreciate it."

Emma eyed the last piece of peach she held. In the firelight, it looked too much like flesh, and she stuffed it back in the baggie of fruit that was still half-full before stretching. "How's Vance doing anyway? You talked to him today before we came back into the woods, it sounded like."

"He's got at least a month of PT, and they'll be monitoring him for any long-term effects of the TBI." Mia winced at the expression on Emma's face. "The doctors are being cautious. He's out of the woods…just not in great shape still. I keep thinking about how close he came to not making it out of that explosion."

Leo's hand froze halfway to his mouth. If he'd fallen back away from the fire off his seat, his reaction to her words couldn't have been clearer.

Seeing him react, Mia suddenly realized what she'd said and jerked straight upright where she sat. "Oh, Leo…" She began to stutter an apology.

He waved her off. "Like I said, guilt."

"I really am sorry."

"No, it's fine. Seriously. We almost lost Vance and Denae, and we both feel responsible, in some way. Survivor's guilt is just another kind of grief, even when the people we thought we'd lost manage to come out alive in the end. We still want to bargain, talk about what could've and should've and would've happened."

Emma rolled her shoulders. "True."

He crumpled the package of nuts into a ball. "You might as well know, both of you, that nearly losing Denae opened up an old wound. I've been thinking a lot about my parents' and grandfather's deaths, and there's no help for it. I know I shouldn't blame myself. But that doesn't mean I don't still do it. I blame myself every day."

Emma was still searching for words when Leo pushed himself to his feet, pocketing the trash he'd been mauling. He muttered something about finding Harley to set up a watch schedule as he disappeared in the direction of their guide's whistling.

Mia gazed after him blankly. "We're all in rough shape right now, aren't we?"

Not quite able to answer, Emma only nodded. The dried fruit had turned sour in her stomach, and all she could do was observe the way the flames fought one another. Another night, she might've thought of them as dancing, but tonight, everything seemed like conflict.

"So...Burt Wilcox is dead, then?"

Emma sat up taller. "Um..."

"Leo told me you called his husband Charlie, like you knew him. I was too hyped up on adrenaline to notice, but that means you saw his ghost. Burt Wilcox is dead. And you *talked* to him."

"I didn't talk to him exactly. But, yeah, he wanted 'Charlie' to know how sorry he was, for dying."

"That's awful." Mia looked as heartbroken as Emma had felt in Burt's presence.

"Yeah, but it got us on this trail, and it's got to be right. I mean—"

"One of the killer's victims directed us here."

"Exactly."

"We have to find Will tomorrow." Mia locked eyes with her.

"We will." She spoke under her breath.

Mia gave her a small nod.

And maybe if we succeed, we'll have the strength to forgive ourselves. For everything.

Emma's mind flitted to the woman her mother's friend Monique had spoken of, but she couldn't let herself go there right now. Not when they had so much else to worry about.

Harley came shuffling back out of the woods with Leo on his heels, but the man had his hands dug into his pockets. He stood by the fire and glared down at it before speaking. "Leo here commented, as we were about to come back up, that he couldn't figure out how nobody knew the Grundys had a boy. I have a confession to make, I guess."

Emma's thoughts of her own problems and Salem vanished into the darkness. This sounded like the beginning of another conversation about guilt.

"I knew that family had a son. Or at least, I suspected it. I'd seen the boy when I'd gone out that way a few times." Harley hunched his shoulders. "When we found the Grundys dead in that house, there were people who wanted to look around, to search for a kid, and I...I said no. I've had a lot of run-ins with Child Services in this part of the state, you want the truth. Once they get their hands into a family, they don't let go."

Emma watched Harley's face. "What did you do?"

Or not do?

"It's like they'd rather see a kid with an abusive foster family than with a biological parent who made a mistake." Harley's brow furrowed into a deep crease. "So...yeah. I don't trust 'em. Figured that if the boy had gone off with family or friends or someone who'd care for 'im, we should just let 'im be. And if he needed the authorities, he'd find his way to us later."

Emma stared at the man, listening to the small noises of the forest around them. "And you didn't...you didn't see him again?"

The ranger shook his head, all but collapsing onto a stone near the fire. "Maybe if I'd looked, put together a search, I could've saved a lot of lives, but I didn't. I'm sorry."

Leo dropped a hand onto the guide's shoulder and patted it, much like he'd gripped Mia's arm earlier. Emma only soaked in the silence surrounding their small fire.

It seemed there had been one boy lost, gone missing a decade ago, and now they had another because of that first disappearance.

She wished she weren't distracted by the thought of what the two of them might be having for dinner tonight, but it was all she could think about.

33

Will's stomach screamed at him for food, but it wasn't in the cards. Not tonight, and not for him.

The man in his father's clothes turned the spit, roasting the dead, headless body. Will felt sick and weak. Hungry while also nauseous and determined never to eat again.

He fingered the remaining baggie of trail rations he'd kept squirreled away in his pocket. The man would toss them into the woods if he found them—he'd told Will the rations he'd carried in his pack weren't fit food for humans—but even if he could've eaten them now, they'd have been little relief.

A few strips of jerky, which he didn't think he could swallow down anyway, and a melted half bar of chocolate and a handful of nuts? The whole of what remained in his pocket would be just enough to light up his taste buds and make him all the hungrier.

The crazy man had been smart enough to share the water Will's dad had stashed at the cabin. They hadn't needed to worry about dehydration, at least. But starvation was another thing. Will's stomach rolled over on itself again.

It doesn't matter that I've barely eaten for the last week. I'm not eating that.

Not a human.

The man grinned, showing off his black teeth in the firelight. "It's ready. What part do you want?"

Will rocked back on his ass, closing his eyes to deny the question. "I'm not hungry."

The man grunted, and Will heard him moving around the fire. Cutting. "I'll have some of the thigh, and so will you."

His boot came down just beside Will, and then a slab of sizzling meat thudded down on the rock to Will's right. His "plate," as the man had called it.

Will couldn't help it. He opened his eyes and glanced down at the blackened hunk. Thigh.

He tore his gaze away from it as fast as he'd looked down. But then what he glimpsed instead was the man tearing into his own large piece of meat. Moisture dripped down his beard, coating his hands.

"You need to eat." The man spoke as he chewed. "You must be hungry, and you need your strength."

"I...can't. It looks too hot anyway. My hands'll burn."

The man paused, staring, and then glanced at his own hands. "You'll get used to it." But unbelievably, he put down his own hunk of meat and leaned over Will's. He cut it into three long strips.

Will swallowed, feeling bile rise through his chest. If only he could reach that jerky in his pocket. But he couldn't go for it with the man watching him. He'd have to get him to look away somehow.

"Eat!"

Will stared at the meat. Finally, he brought himself to touch it. One finger...then two. But he couldn't pick it up. Pulling his hand back, he wrapped his arm back around his knees and shook his head at the man, who wore a deep scowl.

"Your weakness is winning. Okay, do you want to be weak tomorrow? For your next test?" The man tore off another hunk from the thigh in his hand. "There's a test for you in the morning. If you're weak, you will fail. For sure. Okay? Do you want to fail?"

Will remained silent. He tried to make himself touch the meat again but couldn't do it.

"It's a hard test." The man finished the food in his hands, and as he chewed, he reached over with his massive knife and cut one of the chicken-finger-sized pieces of thigh into three more pieces. "Take one bite, and then it will be better. Easier. You don't want to end up like my last son."

I can't do this. I can't do this, but I have to.

Would Dad do it? Mom?

He didn't know the answer to that question...but he knew they'd want him to survive. And thinking of his mother gave him another idea. He'd seen her at the circus, along with the other performers...the ones that were still alive. One of them was a magician, and he'd shown Will how to make a coin disappear by snapping his fingers.

Will had mastered the trick, using it to fool his friends at school. It was his only chance at getting out of this.

With two fingers, he picked up the smallest piece of meat the man had cut apart. He held it above his knees, staring at it, while letting his shirtsleeve slide down to cover his other hand. The man was watching his hand with the meat.

Will opened his mouth, closed it, and then dipped his tongue out to lick his lips. Wetting them so that he could find a voice. "I can't eat it with you watching me."

The man's eyes narrowed on him. "You need to eat, or you will end up like my last son. In a box. Alone."

Swallowing, hard, Will nodded. "I know. Okay. I'll do it."

He turned his other hand palm up and dropped the meat into it, then snapped his other fingers. The man startled. "Why did you do that?"

"I'm just getting myself ready. That's a trick my mom showed me, for taking medicine that tastes bad or when I have to do something I really don't want to do. Okay?"

He snapped again, holding his hand slightly above the meat, but closer than before.

For a moment, Will didn't think the man would fall for it. Finally, though, he brought his hand lower and snapped his fingers as he lifted his other hand, bringing the meat toward his mouth.

He felt the slimy meat falling into his shirtsleeve as he clamped his hand over his mouth and mimicked chewing.

The man clapped his hands. "Good job, son. Good eating. Eat more now, okay?" He reached out and cut another piece for himself, shifting where he sat and turning away to eat.

Will didn't waste a moment. He pretended to swallow, then picked up another piece and set it in his open palm. He snapped his fingers like before as he lifted his hand, making the meat disappear.

The man laughed, but he didn't look at Will. He just kept eating his own meat.

Sliding his hand down to his pocket, Will tugged out a piece of jerky and tucked it into his palm. He reached his other hand out, going for the last piece of meat the man had cut for him.

Quickly, he snatched it up and brought both hands to his mouth, letting the jerky go in while the cooked meat fell into his shirtsleeve to join the other two pieces.

The man across from him chewed and swallowed.

Though the jerky from Will's pocket was fuzzy with lint, he chewed happily.

The man glanced around, as if he expected to see hunks of meat on the ground, but he grinned.

"Good, son. Good. You keep eating."

34

The sun had been up for an hour, and Emma and the others were long since done with breakfast. Shockingly, she'd had a decent night's sleep and been able to eat an MRE and nuts rather than picking at dried fruit.

The emotion of the past night's conversation had, if nothing else, overshadowed the gore of their case and the stress of the missing boy. At least, until she woke up and thought about the day ahead.

They'd already lost two members of their search party. Thinking they could keep everyone safe was naive at best and dangerous at worst. Laurie must still be hanging on, thankfully, but perhaps by a thread.

Leo hefted his pack onto his back. "How is this thing still just as heavy as it was when we started?"

"Always heavier the next day." Mia sipped water before tucking the bottle back into her bag. "Trust me. My dad dragged me on plenty of hikes when I was a kid, and the packs never got lighter, even as the food and water got used up."

One more thing to look forward to, Emma girl.

Emma finished taking a quick catalog of her own remaining supplies while Harley double-checked his own gear.

When he moved back to the trail, searching out signs of boot prints that would match the ones Burt Wilcox had worn —according to his husband—Emma and Leo remained right on his heels. His focus was on tracking, while theirs was on searching out traps.

"Everything okay?" Emma glanced at Harley, who'd just come to a stop in the middle of the trail. "I don't see anythi—"

"Just gimme a second." The ranger studied the foliage surrounding their trail, then pulled out his map and consulted it again. "Burt's a seasoned hiker. Seasoned hikers work to *not* leave traces of themselves. Making sure we're following his path isn't easy."

Emma opened her mouth to retort that she hadn't meant to imply it was, but a quick glance from Leo cut the words off. He was right that snark wasn't going to help anything.

Harley moved forward again, to brush aside branches and overgrowth, and finally let out a sigh. "Someone's already been covering up our hiker's trail, it seems. But this is it."

Barely waiting for Leo and Emma to step in behind him, the tracker stomped forward, eyes on the ground.

They soon fell into the rhythm of the hike, swatting away mosquitoes and trudging along under the weight of their packs. Emma occasionally caught sight of Burt's ghost up ahead and had to bite her lip to stop herself from pushing Harley on. She could only take the ghost's presence as a signal that they were on the right track and perhaps nudge Harley elsewhere if that changed.

An occasional look from Leo and Mia, with a small nod of response from Emma, confirmed that they, too, knew Burt Wilcox was guiding them.

Emma tried not to think too much about the unhappy ending to this story—one that Harley, and most of all, Charlie Renner, weren't privy to yet. She could only hope that Pat Henson hadn't also fallen victim to this serial-killing cannibal. Stopping him and saving Will Payne, hopefully saving Steven Payne, and finding Burt's remains were all they could work toward now.

And she prayed there were no others.

After another few hours of hiking, though, Harley's steps grew slower. Their group hadn't found more traps, but tension had been mounting. Emma could feel it radiating off the man leading them.

"Take a water break, everyone. I need to search for the trail again." Without waiting for a response, he moved off the track.

Emma stepped closer to Leo. "He doesn't sound confident."

"I can hear you!" Harley's shout silenced even the birds, and Emma flinched.

"Sorry, Harley. But if you need more eyes for footpri—"

"I'll damn well say so." He grunted, more like a bear than a man in the moment.

When he'd moved another ten paces into the brush, Leo leaned toward Emma and Mia. "He hasn't been himself since he told us about believing the Grundys had a son. Just let him walk it off."

"Long as he doesn't get himself killed." Mia dropped her pack by her feet and pulled her water bottle free again. "Unless he thinks we found all the traps."

"Not likely." Emma kept her eyes on Harley. It was impossible not to picture what Ben had looked like after falling onto that spiked frame. Not to mention Laurie lying prone on that knife.

Tearing her gaze from their guide, she searched the

surrounding forest for Burt Wilcox. Finally, she found his form off to the left of where Harley was, wavering in the distance. She'd picked up her pack a moment before Harley found the right trail and called them all forward with a tired wave.

"We're on the right track." Emma's whisper drew a quick, searching look from Leo, and she nodded.

Harley led them farther into the woods, seemingly off-trail because it had been so thoroughly covered with new debris. But when he passed by a large tree and turned to follow the newly cleared path, he skidded to a halt. Emma was about to say something when the smell hit her.

Roasted meat, smoke, and a tinge of burned hair.

In a clearing, the body of a man was tied to a spit and hung from a tree high above a firepit. He was headless, and his limbs had been cut off at the elbows and knees so that what remained of him could be tied easily and roasted like a pig.

Marks along one thigh showed where some of his flesh had been cut away recently. After having been cooked, no doubt.

Leo took a heavy step back, cursing, but Emma could only stare.

Beyond the firepit, a small cabin sat still and quiet. Emma nodded toward it, ignoring the body and the pit for the moment. Mia paced alongside her as she made her way forward, but she couldn't imagine there'd be any surprise to their approach if someone was inside.

"FBI! If anyone's inside, come out with your hands up!" Emma's shout echoed over the woods, but other than silencing the birds, it had no effect. She edged closer and peered through the window of the cabin. Inside, a few sleeping bags lay on the floor, and along one wall, she saw a rudimentary sink beside a well-made wooden table. There was no space large enough for a man to hide or even a boy.

She took out her phone and pulled up an image of Steven Payne's diagrams. As best she could tell, the layout of this cabin looked like the one he'd been designing.

"I'm pretty sure this is Payne's hideaway in the woods. It matches up with the drawings we found at his house."

Mia mumbled something about searching around the other side of the cabin, and Emma followed after her with only a backward glance to Leo and Harley, who stood guard over the body.

On the other side of the cabin, Emma nearly stumbled on a head hanging from a tree, covered with flies. Presumably that of the man who'd been roasted over the fire. She swallowed hard to force down the bile in the back of her throat. "How many people has this guy killed?"

Mia swished a branch to scare off the flies long enough so she could photograph the face. "Too many. I don't even recognize this guy from the pictures we've seen of the missing persons."

Emma pushed away the nausea roiling in her stomach and walked the cabin's perimeter until they came back to Leo and Harley.

He glanced over by way of greeting. "Do we think this is Burt Wilcox?"

Emma shook her head, pointing to the man's blackened middle. "Wilcox is skinnier. This is someone else. Plus…we found a head out back. Not Wilcox's, but maybe this guy's."

Taking shallow breaths, she allowed her gaze to linger over the badly burned thighs, where large chunks of flesh had been cut away. Chunks the size of steaks, if she wasn't blind.

Leo bent down to examine the spit more closely, one

hand holding his jacket over his mouth and nose. "I don't think he's more than a couple days dead. He's...not rotting."

"Yet." Emma sighed. "Is the firepit still hot?"

Hovering a hand over the burned wood and ash below the body, Leo shook his head. "No, not hot, but I think it was burning last night."

Mia nodded, taking a step back. "We wouldn't smell the... uh, the body, otherwise."

The cooked meat, she means.

Mia waved her hand at the torso. "What do we do here? We can't...leave him like this. Can we?"

"Let's cover him." Leo stood and headed toward the cabin. "If Jacinda wants to yell at me later about contaminating a scene, let her."

Emma lifted one shoulder in reply to Mia's glance. "We know what killed him or can probably obtain trace DNA from his remains to confirm he's the victim of our cannibal. I'm with Leo."

We just need one last trace to bring him down.

And besides that, the simple truth was that no one should have to look at him—or smell him—any longer. Maybe giving the man some dignity in death was worth breaking protocol, or maybe it wasn't, but Emma had no intention of worrying about that right now.

Her concern was just making sure that nobody else ended up roasting over a fire.

35

I hadn't felt pride in a while, but I did now. And the fact that it was pride in my son meant the world to me. The boy was starting to remind me of myself. Maybe he hadn't eaten much at breakfast, but more connection was coming. He'd get better. And hadn't he done well in helping me cover up our tracks when we left the cabin? If anyone came by while we were gone, they could follow us.

Will understood me when I told him we had to hide from everyone. He helped me move leaves and sticks around to hide our path away from the cabin. That meant something.

We carried rope and tools from the new cabin for Will's next test.

Moving farther into the forest, I stopped at a point where I'd caught a hiker before winter. Behind me, Will came to a slow stop and gazed down at the branches and wooden stakes on the ground. The stakes still showed dried blood along their edges and tips, but most had been broken off the frame I made from branches when the hiker fell on them and died.

"We're going to make this trap new. Fresh. Okay?" I waited for him to nod, and he finally did.

The process was slow. It took time to remove each of the stakes and rebuild the frame. Then we had to cut notches in the stakes and use the rope to fix them on the frame again. But Will worked at it beside me, and the pride I felt grew.

Today was about hunting. Those people we'd seen yesterday would make good meals for *weeks*. Catching and butchering them would be hard work. With me and Will both working, I knew we could succeed.

And then we could get to know those people better. After we were done butchering them and connecting with their flesh, Will and I would be even closer than I'd been to my parents.

We were ready to set this trap, so I arranged the frame with the stakes and trailed out a wire that would make someone fall on it.

"You dig the pit for the frame. Make a shallow hole, so we can put the frame in the ground and cover it with leaves and grass."

He worked slow, but once I had the wire strung, I went to help him.

Together, we got the hole dug and set the frame in place.

With that done, it was time to collect leaves and sticks to cover the trap. I picked up a handful of dry leaves and scattered them over the frame. "You too," I said to Will, "start at the other side."

The boy's eyes were wide, but he finally moved into action and collected handfuls of leaves to sprinkle over the trap.

He still had a lot of fear to overcome, but he worked at it. I thought of what my dad had told me when we'd done our butchering.

"Fear will see you dead, boy. Deader than a doornail. Get over it and get working."

The words came to my tongue, but Will *was* working. Dad hadn't been kind to me...but I could be more patient than him. A better dad.

Bending to my task across from the boy, I focused on covering the spikes. These traps were hard work, but worth the sweat. Worth the effort.

"We'll survive, son."

He grunted in response, but that was fine. He was learning to take care of himself.

Just like I'd learned as a child.

It was a necessary lesson, and the reason my parents had kept me in my room so much as I'd grown. The reason I'd never seen anyone but them 'til near the time they'd died. Sometimes, I'd been lonely. I'd gotten angry at them, even. But they hadn't been bad people...just people doing the best for me that they could.

Will paused, with his hands full of leaves held over a spike that was blood-covered from tip to base.

"Fear will get you killed. Do your job. Now."

"The blood...the blood..." He looked like he might cry. For a second, I wondered if he could be my son, but there wasn't time for that.

I shook him by the shoulder, shaking the tears back into him. "Cover it, then you don't have to see it. Okay? Now!"

The boy's eyes went wide, but he stayed frozen. I released his shoulder and knocked the leaves out of his hands. "Go get more. Do your job!"

He did what he was supposed to. He dropped the rest of the leaves and stomped over to where he'd been collecting them from a pile behind a tree.

"Good son." I nodded at him, watching.

He worked faster now, knowing what he had to do. And in another second, he had it done. "Okay?"

"Good."

I made a point of slowing myself down so he'd get more practice. This was what my dad had done for me. If only I could've known him and my mom better. Known what they were thinking and why they wanted to kill each other.

I wanted to be close to them.

To help them.

Mom hadn't always wanted me to help. She hadn't liked when Dad took me out into the forest to help him with these traps. We'd only been setting traps for animals, but she still complained. Like Dad had said, though, she was as "bloodthirsty" as the rest of us, and never turned down meat when we caught it.

But despite all her protests, we'd connected in the end. Finally.

I'd *learned* connection with their help. Just like Dad must've intended.

After hearing the gunshots, I ran away at first.

That night, I slept in my favorite place in the woods, inside a burned-out tree with moss covering me. I was only eleven, I thought. That was so long ago, I forgot how old I was really, but I knew I was still a boy. Like Will.

Two days passed before I went back to the house, and I only did because I'd been hungry. I ate berries and some small animals I caught and drank from the stream that was flowing near the house. But I was tired of sleeping in the tree, all covered in dirt and with bugs waking me up all the time.

I knew there was still food in the house, and a place to sleep in my room.

Except animals had gotten in and eaten most of the food. The cereal I liked had rat poop in it.

I would never forget how I felt then. Starving and alone. I walked into my parents' room on instinct. Like I always did when I was sad or needed help.

They were lying on the bed, covered in flies and blood. Smelling the blood made me hungry.

Cutting off the parts I ate would've been the hard part. They were Mom and Dad. But animals had found them before I did and had chewed on them. I just did the same thing.

That must've been what Dad planned for me.

He and Mom never liked having me around. That was why they always put me in my room unless it was dinnertime or time to go camping or hunting.

We were never close. But at the end, it was like Dad knew what he had to do to finally get close to me. And they'd done it, and then I'd done what I needed to. And we'd connected.

I shook the thought off. Will didn't need to learn how I'd felt. That was why I hadn't shown him his own dad being butchered. That was my kindness to him, starting us on the right path. Just like my parents must've babied me at first, I babied him. Protected him.

But now we were past that.

After I'd connected with my parents, things got better. They looked just like the animals Dad used to catch, and all I had to do after that was remember what Dad had taught me and copy him. People weren't different than deer or boar or bear.

Will would learn that soon.

He would feel the meat inside him, closer than ever. Connected. Close and connected.

I would spare him years of being alone, living in some old shack with nobody to talk to, making do with hunting little animals and eating what he could find in the woods.

Like I'd done for so long.

Well, until I'd found that lost hiker last year. He said his name was Lenny, and he'd looked so lonely. I'd done him a favor, really.

My connection with him hadn't been what it was with my parents, but it had filled the void inside me. And I felt close to him afterward.

With all the spikes covered, I went to Will and wrapped him in a hug. "Good son. Good, good son. You make me proud."

He muttered, "Thank you," and I stood back to look at him.

I hadn't heard that in a long time.

"Come on. We need to cover more around the trap, so it doesn't look different." I gestured to the forest ground surrounding us. "We want long, skinny branches that are thin and flat. Long grasses." The boy stared, and I hissed at him with a wave of my arm. He stumbled back, eyes to the ground, and we began this part of the hunt. The easy part in terms of sweat, but harder in other ways.

This was where we had to trick our prey.

All those years alone, this was what I'd wanted. A son to do this work with me. To teach some things to, just like my father had taught me.

I dragged branches back to the trap and laid them around it. Will brought some meager ones, and I helped him do the same. We scattered them so the whole area looked natural, like a normal forest trail.

"We deserve a break." I pulled some jerky from my pants and held out one long strip to Will as I bit into another. "Eat this, and then we'll finish."

The boy seemed to shake to pieces before me. He shook his head, and then tears began falling.

"Take it. Eat."

Instead of reaching out to take my offering, he threw back his head and screamed.

The sound split the air between us and around us. Scared every animal. Maybe even sent up an alarm to those people searching for him.

Without thinking, I cuffed him across the face. Hard. He fell sideways, nearly onto the trap, and I grabbed his shirt and pulled him back just in time. "Stop! Okay? Stop that."

His whimper bled into another scream, and I finally reached for him and flattened my palm against his mouth, gagging the noise just like my father had done to me when I'd started screaming at him for hitting Mom.

Will's eyes got bigger, but I held his screams in, feeling his hot panting against my hand. He had to learn.

Maybe he is a bad boy. A good boy wouldn't scream like that.

Screams like that would bring those people with their guns. Those people who wanted to take him from me.

And that couldn't happen. That couldn't happen, and Will had to learn.

It was time to punish my boy before things went wrong. But before I could do that, I felt a stabbing pain in my hip. I let go of Will's mouth on instinct to look down.

The damn boy had stabbed me with the knife from my own trap.

"You're a bad boy now, very bad!"

And bad boys got punished.

36

Emma trudged on behind Harley, sharing a quick look of doubt with Leo. They'd been searching for fresh tracks for a while now. Without any obvious trail to follow, she worried they'd go off course.

Assuming we aren't lost already.

Having a K-9 unit with them would have made their search much easier, but the only ones available were following trails from Steven Payne's truck and so far hadn't reported any success in locating the missing hiker or his son.

Emma, Leo, Mia, and Harley were all still standing—which wasn't nothing—but beyond that, they'd accomplished little since finding the cabin and that roasted hiker. Emma had wanted to leave someone there, to watch the area in case their killer came back.

But Jacinda had been adamant they not split up, and that was one bit of protocol she had no intention of breaking.

Leo sighed beside her. "Harley, are you sure thi—"

A high-pitched scream cut him off. Emma spun in a circle, trying to key in on where exactly it had come from.

The sound broke the morning again, shrill and terrified. He sounded close.

"That has to be Will!" Mia ran one hand through her hair, turning in a circle beside Emma. "Right? I mean—"

Emma gripped her shoulder, pained by the self-doubt bleeding from her voice. "We heard it, too, Mia. Yes, it has to be him."

When the sound came again, they were all ready, and Mia and Emma turned as one in the same direction.

Mia charged first, dropping her pack and running forward at a reckless speed that made Emma's stomach drop even as she hurried forward, eyes on the ground and chasing after her colleague. Leo was beside her, his attention focused on the trees.

They pushed through brush that covered half the trail, calling for Mia to slow down.

"Wait for us! It's not safe."

Harley burst from behind them and was several strides ahead of them in seconds, crashing through the undergrowth after Mia.

She'd vanished into the woods but could still be heard calling for Will even as Harley shouted for Mia to stop.

"You're going to get hurt! Stop moving and wait for us!"

Emma could just make out the shape of his upper body when he suddenly disappeared from view with a rushing sound and rustling of branches.

An agonized groan came from up ahead, and Emma's stomach bottomed out. She charged forward, ignoring the risk. Harley'd been hurt and needed help.

She pulled to a stop at the edge of a steep slope.

At the bottom, Harley lay on his back in a tangled heap, with one leg bent awkwardly to the side. His chest rose and fell with ragged breaths, and he lifted an arm, waving them away.

"Nothing you can do. My leg's broke. Go help the boy."

Leo stumbled to a stop beside Emma. "We go around. There's nothing we can do for him now. Mia's slowed down. She's just up ahead."

As if leading them, another child's scream sounded, but this one bled into a strained whimper and a cry for help. Emma fought back a wave of frustrated tears.

Harley called up to them. "Get moving!"

Emma dropped her pack. She saw no point in being slowed down. Leo kept his, with the extra medical kit it contained.

They moved as fast as was safe until they caught up to Mia. She gave a pained and exasperated groan. "I'm sorry. He's just a boy, and I couldn't just…I had to go after him."

Leo nodded back the way they'd come. "I think we all felt the same way, but Harley's the one who paid for it."

Mia's mouth fell open in shock. "What happened?"

"He went down a steep slope and might have a broken leg. He told us to keep going."

Another pained cry echoed through the woods up ahead, and the three agents refocused on the task of saving Will Payne.

After several steps, the silence had Emma fearing the worst.

A meager whimper put her more at ease, but she still tensed for a fight, on the lookout for signs of the boy. She glanced to Leo and Mia, who had stayed a few paces behind her.

They nodded. They'd heard the noise too.

And then the whimper was suddenly in surround sound.

Emma looked up. The others followed.

Will Payne dangled upside down from a tree branch. His ankles had been lassoed together, and his arms pinwheeled in the air as he swayed from the branch, face turning red with the blood rushing downward. He hovered twelve feet off the ground.

Blood covered one of his hands and the side of his face, but Emma could see no injury on him that might produce such a mess. Will's eyes met hers, went wide, and he screamed anew. "Watch out! Watch out! Behind you!"

Emma drew her gun and whirled, with Leo and Mia fanning out at her back.

She was overwhelmed by a horrific stench. A man crouched right where they'd just been walking, half-hidden by a tree. He couldn't have been older than his twenties, but it was impossible to guess his age, given his condition.

His mouth gaped at her, black teeth giving the impression that he'd been chewing on tar, and blood streaked his clothing and his skin. His matted hair sprouted in all directions, dried with blood and bits of detritus Emma didn't want to bring herself to consider. His eyes were wide and dilated, terrifying…and they were terrified, too, but filled also with some expression Emma couldn't name.

"Don't move," she breathed, raising her weapon as she kept eye contact with him. Behind her, Mia murmured something to the boy, but this bear of a man had her whole focus.

Him, and the long, hand-carved spear trembling in his grip, pointed at her. He was ready to throw.

"Go away. Get away from my son. Okay?" His voice was guttural, scratchy, but the spear steadied as his gaze shot up to Will. "Tell her to get away!"

"Mia." Emma evened her voice, speaking slow. "If Will's okay, let's wait a second. Please."

The man jerked the spear forward but didn't throw it. Yet. "Go away! Okay? Go!"

He sounds just like his parents. This is the Grundys' son.

"We can't go away." Emma held her breath as long as she

could until her lungs screamed at her for relief. She inhaled quickly, trying not to smell the man and the rot surrounding him. Will whimpered above her, and she tried to block out the sound of his pain. "But we can go with the two of you. Take you both somewhere better. So neither of you have to live like this."

The man's brow furrowed, lines of skin accented by blood as he looked back at her in clear confusion.

Will shrieked behind her, "He's not my dad! He's not! I stabbed him in the leg, and he tied me up like this!"

With a snarl, the filthy man yelled curses at Will. "You're a bad son! You won't learn!"

"You're not my dad!"

Leo shushed the boy.

Emma raised her weapon a touch higher, drawing the wild man's attention back to her. "Focus on me, okay? How about you tell me your name?"

His voice scratched out some syllables, but Emma couldn't make them out. She wondered if he even knew his own name anymore, in the state he was in.

The air went cold with the Other, and Emma couldn't help shivering. She glanced to the side, expecting the sad sight of Burt Wilcox, but it was the Grundys.

"Dale is a bad boy. A very, very bad boy." Alan Grundy shook his head, staring at his apparent son. "He should go back to the closet where he belongs. Before he screws up anything else."

Emma swallowed against the hate radiating from the couple and looked back at the man in front of her, Dale. He looked more like a caveman from comic books than any man she'd seen in recent times.

A thick stain of blood covered his right hip, fresh and oozing all over his grimy pants. He leaned to the other side, favoring his right leg.

The rest of the blood on him, including the stains wreathing his lips and arms, was dried. Despite the injury he'd suffered, his grip on the spear was steady as he aimed directly at her. She imagined he knew how to hit his mark.

"Dale. That's your name?" Emma ignored the deep breath Leo took behind her and took the tiniest of steps closer to that deadly spear. "Will is a good boy. Not a bad boy."

His eyes remained on her, but he scowled, hiding those dark, rotted teeth for a moment before he answered her. "No. I thought my son…was a good boy, but I was wrong. He's bad. He brought you here."

The man's fist reared back on that note, preparing to throw the spear, but not at Emma. Will was his target.

Emma fired, and blood spurted from the man's throwing arm as he stumbled to the side and turned. He ran clumsily, crashing through the wilderness, heading in the direction of the cabin.

"Mia, help Will!"

And then Emma was running after the man, Leo on her heels.

Behind her, Will screamed out yet another warning. "There's traps! Be careful!"

Emma skidded to a halt before taking careful steps forward, looking for tracks the man had left behind as she pressed into the underbrush.

She could only hope he knew where he'd set his own traps and wouldn't draw all three of them to their deaths.

37

My breath crashed in and out of my lungs, and I felt wetness scarring my face. Dad would've hated me right now, but I couldn't stop.

I couldn't stop running. I couldn't stop crying. I couldn't stop hating myself and my son. Will had grabbed the knife in my own trap when I'd pushed him so close to it.

Then he stabbed me with it!

Those people with their guns should not have come to my forest. They were the reason my son turned on me. My hip and arm throbbed, pain shooting down from the bullet wound and where Will had hurt me. But I couldn't stop to help myself. I had to get away. From them.

How had my son betrayed me like this?

He'd done so well. Building the spit and helping me with the traps. And he'd even been eating the meat, learning to connect.

I'd been so happy. So proud. Ready to teach him more.

My foot caught on one of my own wires, and I jumped straight up and out of it with a scream, nearly tripping one of our fresh traps. I caught myself, just in time, saving the trap too.

And then I ran on.

But maybe it would've been better if I'd fallen on that knife. Died right there. Tears burned at the thought, but it was true. I'd been so wrong.

The forest blurred around me. I'd been so excited to teach Will more. What a smart boy he'd turned out to be, and I'd taught him so well already. We'd only needed more time.

Why had he stabbed me? Why had he screamed and brought the people with guns? The people wanting to separate us…right when we'd started to connect. Now those people had him.

My son's not safe. Both of us are unsafe.

The people meant to hurt my son and me both. All I'd ever wanted was to be close to my boy, and the people inside me. Inside us.

I'd done good. I was good. Why was this happening?

Tears choked me. I tripped and just let myself fall forward, but there was no trap to catch me. Must've been a tree root. I righted myself and ran on.

Why didn't my son love me?

My dad's voice echoed in my head. *"You're not good enough! How could I love you?"*

I screamed back at him, rage burning up my throat. "I was good enough! He was going to love me!"

Damn emotion made me lose my balance, and I banged the arm that had gotten shot against a tree. It hurt bad, and so did my hip. I almost fell again and wanted to stop, but I had to run.

My dad wasn't right. I'd find a new son if I had to. Someone who'd learn and be good and connect with me and love me. Even if the people with guns had Will.

I could find a new son.

They wanted to hurt me, but they wouldn't catch me. Too many traps between me and the house, and only two of them were running after me. I'd catch them, and then I'd eat them and connect with them too. Maybe then they'd know me. Know what they'd ruined. That would be okay.

Every time I ate someone, I got closer to them. Maybe I'd know why they'd wanted to take my son, just like they'd know me. We'd all be closer. Maybe the connection wouldn't even go away this time.

I'll know someone. Many someones.

Dad was wrong. He was wrong when he said I'd never know anything or anyone.

Despair tore at me, through my arm and my tears. I couldn't be bad. Not after all this time.

But my parents' voices echoed after me in the woods, drowning out the running steps of the people with guns.

"You're a bad boy, Dale! A bad boy! A very bad boy!"

Another scream built in my throat, and I let it out, burning up with the emotion as I ran. Those people with guns wouldn't win.

I wouldn't let them.

38

Emma stumbled when the air went cold.

Leo caught her arm and pulled her up. "Careful."

Ghosts suddenly swooped forward, flanking them, and Emma slowed to take them in. Burt Wilcox and another man who was covered in blood. She was about to open her mouth to tell Leo when the ghosts ran ahead, moving like the wind. When they stopped dead, gesturing so wildly that blood flew off into the air from the motion, Emma skidded to a halt. "Leo, wait!"

He turned to her, just short of where Burt Wilcox loomed ahead of him. "What?"

Throat dry, Emma hurried forward to stand beside him and searched the ground at Burt's feet. Her skin rose in goose bumps as the man nodded, wide-eyed. "There, look."

A wire ran between two trees, just ahead of the ghost's feet, covered with leaves. Emma followed it over to a tree some five feet off the path and traced it up until she came to the board with sharpened branches sticking out from it.

Leo blanched. "Shit. How did you even see it?"

But Emma had already stepped over the wire and hurried

toward the next ghost who'd stopped, a tattooed stranger who appeared to have been stabbed to death. He had his arms spread wide, and Emma immediately saw the trip wire behind him and the knife jutting up from the ground. This was the same sort of trap that had caught Laurie.

She turned back to Leo, who'd followed her steps and stood right behind her, a confused grimace on his face. "Ghosts." Her voice croaked, and she faced the ghost who'd alerted her to the wire. "They're stopping at the traps, showing us what to avoid. Let me lead?"

"Burt Wilcox?"

"And another guy."

A ragged breath came from his lips, and he gave a terse nod. "We need to hurry, though."

When Emma turned back around, Burt was already a few dozen paces farther into the trees, and the tattooed ghost had also moved forward. Taking a careful step over the wire and then hopping over the readied spears, she focused more on the ghosts than the ground.

"We should disable these traps," Leo panted as he ran after her, "for anyone following behind us."

Emma agreed, but the sound of their killer crashing through the brush ahead drew her on. "You take care of that. I'll follow our 'guides' and keep after Dale Grundy."

Leo begrudgingly accepted her suggestion and set to dismantling the traps they'd found.

The ghosts hopscotching ahead of her seemed to approve, the way they led her on.

Burt and the other ghost both came to a stop together a ways ahead, and Emma slowed her pace. Closer up, she found they'd stopped at the edge of a pit. Heart thumping, she kicked at the loose branches, sending them tumbling downward. A glance over the edge showed a dozen spikes that had been waiting for an unwary victim.

She moved into the woods, pacing along the side of it before she came back to the relatively open trail they'd been following. Their killer was ahead—she could hear him—and for whatever reason, he'd slowed down.

Leo trotted up behind her, gesturing through the trees. "He's headed back to the cabin. Gotta be."

The ghosts were ahead, and Emma made sure she and Leo avoided the traps, giving him time to reveal trip wires or trigger them without putting either of them in danger.

A door slammed somewhere ahead, signaling how close they were to the cabin. Though it hadn't felt like it, they'd made a big circle in the Buckskin Wilderness, proof of how easy it was to get lost.

When she and Leo came out into the clearing, the sleeping bag Leo had thrown over the roasted body sat between them and the structure like a red warning flag, all the ghastlier because they knew what lay underneath it. Emma and Leo walked around it on opposite sides, guns up, and came within a few dozen feet of the door before Emma spoke.

"FBI! We know you're in there! Dale, you need to come out now, hands up!"

A shadow moved past the rough opening for a window inside the newly erected cabin, and then a fist appeared... holding a head. The hand hurled the head out the window at them, and Emma leaped to the side. The head landed and rolled, coming up against the sleeping bag behind them.

Emma's stomach flipped over as she glanced at the head. Eyes open, it stared at her. A trail of dried blood ran down from one side of its lips. Some sort of fluid trailed out of one ear, and rot could be seen spreading along the skin. She almost expected it to blink, but thankfully, that didn't happen.

She recognized the face, though. It matched an image

she'd been looking at just a couple of days earlier, when the case began. "That's Steven Payne."

Leo swallowed, visibly, and nodded. "We should go in before he throws anything else at us. Body parts are one thing, but spears and knives are another."

"Were there any weapons inside when you went in to get that sleeping bag?"

He shook his head. "Nothing I could see, but that doesn't mean anything. He could've kept a stash hidden anywhere, outside or in."

"Just wait." She sighed, searching for more movement along the window. "He could be crouched in there with a spear or knife, just waiting for us to open that door. I want to try something else first."

The memory of his parents and their cruel words had been playing in her mind on repeat, and she couldn't get their refrain out of her head. If she channeled them and acted out an opposite role, maybe they'd get somewhere.

"Dale, listen to me!" Emma tried to soften her voice, projecting. "I know you're a good boy. So does my friend. You're a very good boy, and nobody's going to make you go into a closet ever again!"

She could feel Leo's eyes burrowing a hole into the side of her head. Emma knew he wanted to end the standoff as quickly as possible, but she had to keep trying. Dale could be brought in without using more force.

She had to believe that, even if Dale himself probably didn't.

Not yet anyway.

"Your parents were wrong, Dale. They thought you were bad, but we know you're good. We know you are. Nobody's going to make you be alone again."

Very likely a lie, but one I can live with.

She waited through the silence, and was just about to

continue when his croaking, scratching voice sounded out. "I don't want to go back in the closet. Not any closet. That's a bad place."

A sigh left Leo, but he didn't lower his gun even a touch. Beside him, Emma felt her own adrenaline speeding. Her negotiation efforts would pay off…she just needed Dale to meet her in the middle.

"You're never going to have to go there again, Dale." She tried to channel Mia's softness as she went on, cajoling. "There's such a big world outside this forest. People you can meet and get to know if you want to. No closets, no bad stuff, no bad people for you to worry about. You won't have to be alone."

"I'm not alone!" The man's scream echoed around the clearing, desperate. "I had my son, but you took him!"

Leo cursed under his breath. "Shit."

Shaking her head, Emma stepped closer to the house. They were so close to getting him to back down, she could feel it. "Dale, you know better. You're smart. That boy back there isn't your son. He's going to leave these woods too."

For a moment, Emma thought she'd gone too far and that she'd have been better off tempting him with the idea of returning Will to his side, but then a loud sob broke out. Wails of pent-up emotion reverberated from the cabin.

The door creaked open a few inches, and a small surge of relief shot through Emma. But the feeling was short-lived. Dale's wails turned to an animalistic growl just as the door was thrown open.

Dale charged out, wild-eyed, with a rusted axe clutched in both hands.

"Get back!" Leo shouted, raising his gun.

But Emma was already moving, her instincts kicking in. She aimed and fired, the shot ringing out through the clearing. The bullet struck Dale in the shoulder, sending him stumbling backward. His grip on the axe faltered, and it crashed to the ground as he crumpled to his knees, clutching his wound.

Emma's heart pounded as she approached cautiously, gun still trained on Dale. He was rocking back and forth, muttering to himself.

"I'm a good boy…I'm a good boy…I'm a good boy…"

Leo moved in quickly, securing Dale's hands behind his back after tossing the axe out of the man's reach. Emma's pulse was still racing, but as she watched Dale, now whimpering on the ground, a mixture of pity and revulsion competed with each other.

"It's over." Leo's voice held the same edge of uncertainty Emma felt. Dale continued to murmur under his breath, his words blending into the eerie stillness of the forest.

Was it? Emma wasn't sure.

39

Monique sat in her garden with her hands dug into the soil around her, eyes closed. In her mind's eye, she watched Emma. The woman was the warrior version of her mother, Gina, chasing a feral, insane killer through the Virginia woods while avoiding deadly traps as if it were just another day at the office. She supposed it was, for Emma. The woman was so successful, but still, the sight remained shocking.

Through the ghosts, she'd caught close-up glimpses of her friend's daughter in action. These denizens of the Other had helped Emma, though for the sake of revenge or generosity, Monique couldn't guess. What mattered, though, was that they allowed her to keep watch.

Watching her hunt the killer, Monique couldn't help marveling over how brave she was. Strong-willed and powerful, like Gina had always been, and just as clever.

I hope she'll trust me. Though I wouldn't blame her if she didn't. She doesn't really know me from Eve.

Monique took a deep breath of the rosemary-scented air, centering herself as Emma left her view. She kept her eyes closed, though, treasuring the bond she'd had with the young woman, however brief it had been.

She only hoped she'd gotten through to her in that brief conversation they'd managed.

A yawn built up in her chest, and she gave in to the impulse. But the thought of napping didn't appeal to her, and she forced her eyes open, attempting what calm she could find.

The wolf's howls had kept her up last night, unwilling to leave her alone, haunting her every dream. Monique's lifelong enemy must've realized she made contact with Emma.

Her spell of protection had held this long, and that had to mean something. The idea of it failing now, at the most disastrous time possible, felt like too much to bear.

Emma had to come home to Salem soon.

I can't take much more of these dreams. Not if I want to stay sane.

Opening herself up to the Other one more time, Monique reached out to the surrounding ghosts. Chanting beneath her breath, she opened herself to the spirits and waited.

Her hope was to reconnect with Emma just once more, to convince her to come to Salem.

But it wasn't Emma's face that appeared in her vision. It was the other woman, the one she and Gina had once called a friend.

The enemy.

The woman grinned, her sadistic smile spreading across her face like a virus. "Your time is running out, Monique. I'm coming for you." She giggled, eyes flashing. "I'm coming for *both* of you."

40

Emma finished describing the collection of body parts they'd fished from Steven Payne's cabin. Some had been collected from a lined compartment beneath the floor, which Payne had constructed for storing perishable food safely. Still other body parts had come from the surrounding woods. Across the conference table from her, Jacinda's mouth hung open with shock.

Mia winced. "We still don't know how many different people all the parts belong to, between Payne's cabin and the old one where Dale lived before. They've identified twelve different sets of remains so far, but the coroner I spoke to didn't seem confident that'll be the end of it."

Leo sipped from his coffee cup. "I could live to be a hundred and never forget this case. I wish I could forget it tomorrow, though."

"I'm just glad you're all safe." Jacinda combed her fingers through her hair, gaze coming to rest on Mia. "Talk about a first case back."

Mia let out a long sigh. "If I could go back in time, I might take another day."

"Don't even think it." Emma glared at her in jest. "It took every one of us on watch to survive that."

Jacinda shook her head, pushing away a file as if to change the subject. "Speaking of, I got word from the sheriff's office that Ranger Laurie Mason may actually pull through. She's still in critical condition, but the doctors have more optimism than they did initially. Same with her supervisor, Ben Carter. And Harley too. His leg was broken in three places, but he'll recover."

Emma sighed and leaned back in her chair, picturing the way Laurie, Harley, and Ben had looked the last time she'd seen any of them. Bleeding, broken, or both. But she was glad she hadn't seen any of their ghosts turn up.

Jacinda reached out and gripped Emma's hand, drawing her gaze. "Emma, you all did everything you could. I can't imagine how horrifying this case must've been. Fortunately, your shots didn't result in a fatality."

"Small mercies, I guess."

The SSA smiled. "Your administrative leave extends until next Friday. We'll come back together after that, as a team." She glanced around the table, meeting each of their eyes in turn. "Today's Friday. You have the weekend off, and Leo and Mia…if you need more time than that, I think I can arrange it. If anyone argues, showing them some choice crime scene photos should manage the trick."

"Can we *not* see those photos?" Leo shook his head and pushed his coffee away. "Just the thought of the CSI team having to go out there and catalog all that…"

"It's going to take a while to process everything." Jacinda nodded at the file, her voice bleeding sympathy. "But considering that Dale confessed to all the murders and explained about his so-called 'connections,' the case is cut-and-dried at this point. Hopefully, you won't have to linger over the pictures or paperwork. Speaking of, did I tell you the police down there found a homemade birth certificate for our killer?"

Emma had to laugh, thinking of the feral man. "Why am I not surprised?"

Jacinda's eyes went softer, and she nodded. "There was no official record of Dale Grundy in hospital or county records. Nobody in town seems to have heard of him, so the parents must've worked hard to keep him isolated."

"He seemed more confused than anything when we arrested him." Emma stretched her fingers, trying to forget the feel of his clothing and the dried blood she'd been unable to avoid touching as they'd cuffed him and stood him up. "Kept asking if he was a bad boy, all the way out of the woods, and not saying much else. Talking about his *connections*."

"It's tragic." Jacinda seemed to wilt in her seat before deciding to continue. "But remember, you saved Will Payne. And we alerted his mother that it looks like her ex-husband really was just taking their son out hiking. We'll know more after the autopsy, but one of the CSI team reported finding a lot of skin under Payne's fingernails and bruises on his body. He seemed to think Steven fought like hell to protect his kid. I hope that gives her some comfort, even if she didn't know about his TBI."

"That kid's got a long recovery ahead of him." Leo toyed with his coffee cup, staring at the liquid. "I know he's with a psychologist now, waiting on being released to his mother, but he'll be haunted forever."

"At least he's alive and physically unharmed," Jacinda spoke quietly, the reminder hanging between them, "and that's due to the boy having some survival tactics of his own, and thanks to the three of you. Now get on out of here. Rest."

Emma shoved herself up to standing. She was sore and

stiff, but more than that, weighed down with everything. The case as well as her mother's friend.

Outside Jacinda's office, she led the way to their desks and glanced around to make sure they were alone before turning to Leo and Mia. They looked exhausted. Mia was still drawn from her ordeal with the kidnappers, and the time spent escorting Will out of the woods seemed to have drained Leo in a way Emma hadn't seen before. It took her back to the conversation they'd had about survivor's guilt, and she wished she could just wave goodbye to the two of them and say she'd see them Monday after they all slept the sleep of the good.

But things weren't that simple.

"I'm really proud of both of you." Her voice caught with emotion, but she pushed past it. "I know how hard this case was on all of us, but we stayed together. We're here because we relied on each other and trusted each other."

Leo's lips flashed the tiniest of grins. "And your 'friends.'"

Emma sucked on her lower lip, but finally nodded. "But the point remains, we did good. We held up, even with just the three of us out there. And, yes, you trusted my 'friends.'" Which meant they trusted her ability explicitly. It was hard to put that kind of gratitude into words. "That means everything to me. I just wanted you both to know that."

Mia flushed. "Shucks, Emma, you want us to cry?" She pulled her into a fast hug that didn't last nearly long enough. "And…"

Blinking at her, Emma waited for the finish and only spoke when it didn't come. "And what?"

"And there's something else coming." Leo perched on his desk, crossing his arms over his chest. "We can see it on your face, so spit it out."

"Right." Emma laughed. The two of them knew her so well…maybe better than anyone else had ever known her.

"I'm going to Salem. ASAP, maybe tomorrow if I can get some sleep tonight. This is my chance, since I'm on leave anyway. If you want to come, you can."

Leo resettled himself on his desk, getting comfortable. "This is where you tell us what happened when you passed out?"

Emma nodded, and leaned in closer to fill them in on everything. On Monique, the ghosts she'd been accosted by in her vision when they'd spoken, and everything the woman had told her.

When she finished, silence blanketed the moment.

Leo finally spoke up. "I'm coming with you. Whether it's tomorrow or not, I'm coming."

"Me too." Mia made a pointed glance toward her go bag, still sitting on her own desk. "Every step of the way, Emma, I'm with you. And whenever you want to leave, we're ready. Jacinda said we can have some time off. I say we're all due for a vacation."

Emma felt emotion trying to push its way up her throat, but this time, she didn't try to hide it. With the three of them together, maybe she had a chance to stave off that wolf after all.

41

Emma packed her best sneakers and her only remaining pair of hiking boots into her suitcase, pushing them down tight.

The other pair had been collected as evidence because of blood spatter on them. And given that Emma hadn't even been able to say whose blood that was…well, that had seemed like reason enough to hand them over without protest.

Maybe she'd just leave them in some dusty evidence bin forever, after the way the last week had gone.

With her suitcase full, Emma finally turned to the picture of herself and her mother that lived on her nightstand. The past several days had taken her away from the apartment, and when she came back, the picture had been standing upright.

This morning, as she'd woken up, the picture had been lying face down. Emma's gut told her she might need the photograph. For centering herself in the present if nothing else, little as that might make sense to someone outside her life. This photo had been with her everywhere.

And considering that it felt like her entire life had been

leading up to this trip, this moment, it only made sense to bring the picture, along with the one she'd found showing her mother and her two friends. She tucked that one into the back of the picture frame.

After covering the photos with two sweaters, she zipped up her suitcase. Across town, she figured Mia and Leo were doing the same.

She wondered if they had as many questions as she did right now. They seemed never-ending.

Would she still be able to see ghosts and hear them if they managed to stop the mystery woman? And what was Monique really capable of?

Not to mention the glaring question that surmounted them all. What was this other woman planning, and would they be able to stop it? Let alone stop it without any of them getting injured? The fact that Emma didn't even know what sort of danger she was putting her friends in was enough to make her want to crawl into her bed and hide.

But she couldn't do that, just like she couldn't refuse Leo's and Mia's willing offers of help.

Because if this witch was as powerful as Monique had said and was planning something big, there was no telling how many people might be in danger.

Her cell rang from where it sat charging on the nightstand, and Esther's number stared up at her. Emma picked up the phone after a moment of hesitation. She'd been expecting the call but couldn't imagine what the woman was going through.

"Hi, Esther."

"Emma. Emma, thank you." The woman sniffled, betraying the fact that she'd been crying. "I can't thank all of you enough for saving my Will. I hear that poor Steven tried, but I wouldn't even have Will back if not for you. Thank you so, so much."

"Of course. That's our job." Emma waited while the woman's crying calmed a touch, then added, "Will seems like a really brave kid. He's going to be okay."

"He—" Esther's voice cut off suddenly.

Emma's heart sped up just a touch. It had been as if someone cut off the fortune teller's air, the way she'd stopped. "Esther, are you okay? Are you there?"

"The streets of Salem will run red with blood." The voice on the other end of the line was no longer Esther's.

Emma's whole body chilled.

Some deeper and darker presence had taken over Esther Payne. "The wolf's howl will fill the world forever. Salem is only the beginning."

Emma searched for words, but it was too late.

The fortune teller hung up, and Emma was left listening to silence. Her own blood ran colder and colder beneath her skin as she stared at her phone in shock.

I never told her about Salem.

Emma swallowed the realization, fighting off chills. She had to go.

She had to go *now*.

The End
To be continued...

Thank you for reading.
All of Emma Last series books can be found on Amazon.

ACKNOWLEDGMENTS

The past few years have been a whirlwind of change, both personally and professionally, and I find myself at a loss for the right words to express my profound gratitude to those who have supported me on this remarkable journey. Yet, I am compelled to try.

To my sons, whose unwavering support has been my bedrock, granting me the time and energy to transform my darkest thoughts into words on paper. Your steadfast belief in me has never faltered, and watching each of you grow, welcoming the wonderful daughters you've brought into our family, has been a source of immense pride and joy.

Embarking on the dual role of both author and publisher has been an exhilarating, albeit challenging, adventure. Transitioning from the solitude of writing to the dynamic world of publishing has opened new horizons for me, and I'm deeply grateful for the opportunity to share my work directly with you, the readers.

I extend my heartfelt thanks to the entire team at Mary Stone Publishing, the same dedicated group who first recognized my potential as an indie author years ago. Your collective efforts, from the editors whose skillful hands have polished my words to the designers, marketers, and support staff who breathe life into these books, have been instrumental in resonating deeply with our readers. Each of you plays a crucial role in this journey, not only nurturing my growth but also ensuring that every story reaches its full potential. Your dedication, creativity, and finesse have been nothing short of invaluable.

However, my deepest gratitude is reserved for you, my beloved readers. You ventured off the beaten path of traditional publishing to embrace my work, investing your most precious asset—your time. It is my sincerest hope that this book has enriched that time, leaving you with memories that linger long after the last page is turned.

With all my love and heartfelt appreciation,

Mary

ABOUT THE AUTHOR

Mary Stone

Nestled in the serene Blue Ridge Mountains of East Tennessee, Mary Stone crafts her stories surrounded by the natural beauty that inspires her. What was once a home filled with the lively energy of her sons has now become a peaceful writer's retreat, shared with cherished pets and the vivid characters of her imagination.

As her sons grew and welcomed wonderful daughters-in-law into the family, Mary's life entered a quieter phase, rich with opportunities for deep creative focus. In this tranquil environment, she weaves tales of courage, resilience, and intrigue, each story a testament to her evolving journey as a writer.

From childhood fears of shadowy figures under the bed to a profound understanding of humanity's real-life villains, Mary's style has been shaped by the realization that the most complex antagonists often hide in plain sight. Her writing is characterized by strong, multifaceted heroines who defy traditional roles, standing as equals among their peers in a world of suspense and danger.

Mary's career has blossomed from being a solitary author to establishing her own publishing house—a significant milestone that marks her growth in the literary world. This expansion is not just a personal achievement but a reflection of her commitment to bring thrilling and thought-provoking stories to a wider audience. As an author and publisher, Mary continues to challenge the conventions of the thriller genre, inviting readers into gripping tales filled with serial killers, astute FBI agents, and intrepid heroines who confront peril with unflinching bravery.

Each new story from Mary's pen—or her publishing house—is a pledge to captivate, thrill, and inspire, continuing the legacy of the imaginative little girl who once found wonder and mystery in the shadows.

Connect with Mary online

- facebook.com/authormarystone
- x.com/MaryStoneAuthor
- goodreads.com/AuthorMaryStone
- bookbub.com/profile/3378576590
- pinterest.com/MaryStoneAuthor
- instagram.com/marystoneauthor

Printed in Great Britain
by Amazon